"Tell me you're intrigued," he said

Greg's hands were sliding up and down her arms, slowly and gently. She tried to breathe, but there suddenly didn't seem to be enough oxygen in the air. His hand slid up to her shoulder, then his fingers spread around the base of her neck, his thumb pressing her chin upward.

He doesn't have a serious thought in his head, Anne warned herself. *All he cares about is drinking and smoking and gambling and picking up women in bars. He is a far cry from the man of your dreams.*

As his mouth moved against hers, so persuasive and warm, it sent a thrill of longing through her that she was not sure she could contain. Her hands lifted to his chest, her fingers pressed against the soft material of his shirt.

No, he was wrong for her. But yes—heaven help her—she was intrigued.

ABOUT THE AUTHOR

Andrea Davidson began her writing career with
the American Medical Association in Chicago
and then, after the birth of her first child, wrote
on a free-lance basis. A seasoned romance
author, also writing under the pseudonym Elise
Randolph, Andrea now resides in Houston,
Texas, with her husband and two children.

Books by Andrea Davidson

HARLEQUIN AMERICAN ROMANCE

These books may be available at your local bookstore.

Don't miss any of our special offers. Write to us at the
following address for information on our newest releases.

Harlequin Reader Service
P.O. Box 52040, Phoenix, AZ 85072-2040
Canadian address: P.O. Box 2800, Postal Station A,
5170 Yonge St., Willowdale, Ont. M2N 6J3

An Unexpected Gift

ANDREA DAVIDSON

Harlequin Books

TORONTO • NEW YORK • LONDON
AMSTERDAM • PARIS • SYDNEY • HAMBURG
STOCKHOLM • ATHENS • TOKYO • MILAN

Published October 1985

First printing August 1985

ISBN 0-373-16122-0

Chapter One

The tremendous crash of hollow horns came to Anne across the craggy, windswept face of the mountain, scattering over the high bench still glazed with patches of snow, and reverberating up to the narrow ledge where she sat cross-legged with a notebook in her lap, a biscuit in her hand, and a tin of beef open and half-eaten beside her. She raised her head and listened. It came again, distinct and resounding and frighteningly masculine. The restless and formidable signal of a rutting ram.

Staying low against the talus of fallen rocks, she slipped quickly but quietly along the granite ridge, gray and glaring under the noonday sun. Up this high, there were few trees, but she tried to stay behind cover of the gnarled krummholz and scrub pine that threw cool, slanted lines of shadows across the ledge. A white-tailed ptarmigan, still wearing its snowy camouflage coat of winter plumage, was feeding on a newly flowered dryad about ten feet away; Anne paused, wondering if she should take the time to photograph the bird. She brushed back a strand of thick brown hair from her face and tucked it into the band at the back of her head. She really should try to get a picture; she hadn't seen too many of the birds this summer. But she would have to remove her pack and take out the camera, and that might startle the sheep. No, she didn't want to lose the ram. His behavior was too critical to her scientific study. She had to keep moving.

On a jutting point above the cliff she passed a slight depression in the rock's shale surface and noticed the fresh droppings. It was the ram's home. He had scraped at the dirt with a hoof to make a slight smooth hollow. Here he had bedded down for the night, and today he was moving on. She followed the animal tracks, blunt and rectangular in the loose dirt, until they disappeared again on the hard stone.

The forceful sound continued, a sharp thwack, like an ax smiting a giant fir tree. Anne sucked in a cold, dry breath and held it when her foot slipped on a wet, lichen-covered rock, causing some loose pieces of granite to slide down the bluff. She hunkered down low against the scrubby vegetation and scooted across the precipice, hoping her mottled brown jacket would blend with the landscape. Vision was the bighorn's most important and acute sense—eight times superior to that of man—and she knew if she were not careful, he would spot her and tear off through the trees.

She squatted with one knee resting on the rocky ledge and carefully pulled her Bushnell scope from

the pack. A furry yellow-bellied marmot was bask-
ing on a sun-drenched boulder a few feet away, but
it woke up and spotted Anne. Praying it wouldn't
take a notion to scream, as they so often did when
frightened, she was vastly relieved when, after
staring at her for a moment, it slowly waddled back
under the protective cover of the rocks.

She lifted her telescope, scanning every craggy
peak and rocky knoll around. Finally she spotted
him. He was several hundred yards away and lower
than she was, shaded somewhat by the overhanging cliff. He was a huge animal, weighing probably
as much as three hundred pounds, with a white
rump and a puny rope of black tail. For his morning feed he had gone down to a sub-alpine pasture
deep in sweet grasses and flowers. Through the
middle of the meadow ran a stream, its clay banks
rich with salt.

But the ram was not feeding or drinking now and
this is what had drawn Anne's attention in the first
place. The echoing crash came again and she
watched mesmerized as this great mountain animal repeatedly charged with his horns into a huge
granite boulder.

The thunderous crash most likely could be heard
for a mile or more, and despite the fact that she felt
something vaguely disturbing and almost too personal about the behavior, the scientist in her blessed
her good fortune that she was here to witness this
magnificent sight. And, too, it would add an interesting footnote to her file. For this was the middle
of June and the mating season for the Rocky

Mountain bighorn was October to December. Banging horns, she knew, was often an audible marking of territory, but that was usually done during the season of rut.

She lowered her scope and sat back against the warm, sunbaked rocks, letting all the behavioral possibilities and educated guesses as to the ram's actions fill her mind. She opened her journal and began to write, but stopped when the sound came again. The utter force and strength of it shook her to the core of her being. She didn't want to feel anything. She didn't want any personal thoughts to intrude. She wanted to remain totally objective and untouched by this.

The professional in her took over and began to write in the notebook. One thing was clear: Even within a species whose cycles were as predictable as the changing seasons, there were always anomalies. There were those singular creatures who by their inexplicable behavior scorned the textbooks that had been written to contain them.

This one ram—full grown by the size of his massive full curl of horns—whose biological clock was obviously out of kilter, had broken away from the small herd of rams he usually summered with high in the alpine meadows and was now battering his horns, a randy male in desperate need of a mate.

Anne Holdenfield, the twenty-nine-year-old biologist who had lost in love more times than she cared to remember, and who, in the process, had also lost the responsive woman within, remained closed and hardened to the phenomenon before her.

Only Anne the scientist opened herself enough to raise the scope again and watch, smiling at this gift of nature so rare, so unexpected.

THE YOUNG, BLOND and exquisitely proportioned coed walked past the booth where the five men were drinking pitcher after pitcher of cold draft beer, and Greg Fisher went through exaggerated motions of banging his head against the wall.

His colleague and friend, Al Kanook, laughed and grabbed his arm. "Later, old buddy. You can take care of your sex life in a little while. First things first."

Greg tore his eyes away from the girl and took a hefty swig of his beer, then lit a cigarette off the one he had just finished. "I can't do this," he said through a haze of smoke as his eyes circled the group. Next to him was Al and across the table were three graduate students. "What is all this hogwash anyway?"

A. J. Bertram leaned his elbows on the table. "Look, Dr. Fisher, you're the one who's always claiming that you have to live history to make it come alive."

Greg picked up his beer mug and analyzed the clarity of its gold color in the soft light. "I said that?"

"All the time," the students agreed. "And you also spent thirty minutes of class time one day boasting that you could find this lost mine. 'Research,' you said. 'All it takes is a little research. Any moron could do it,' you said."

Greg flicked the ashes from his cigarette, but they didn't quite make it into the ashtray. He glanced at Al. "Are they serious?"

"I think so. Here, have some more beer."

Greg watched as the last drop from the pitcher was drained into his mug. Al ordered another one, their fourth or fifth. They had all lost count at this point. Tomorrow was the first day of the summer session, and for the first time since he received his post at Princeton ten years ago, Greg Fisher was not going to teach a class. He was taking a break for the summer. He wasn't going to work; he was going to play. It had seemed like such a good idea at the time he made the decision, an easy, relaxing change of pace. No deadlines, no lectures, no papers to grade, no thickheaded little skulls to try to penetrate. But now he questioned the decision. The long dry months ahead loomed like an endless stretch of desert, and he was beginning to wonder how on earth he was going to occupy his time.

A group of young women walked by and a couple of them smiled beguilingly at him. He recognized them from the last semester. In fact, he thought he had taken one of them out a couple of times. He couldn't remember for sure. After ten years of one-night stands, all those pretty young faces and bodies were starting to blend together into a shapeless blur.

Greg watched the girls as they found a table nearby. Hm, he thought. The long summer might hold some promise after all, and maybe there were still a few surprises to be found. He certainly wasn't ready to give up the fun of looking. And that tall one over there with the long dark hair probably spelled fun with a capital *F*. What the hell, he could probably talk her into going home with him. What else did he have to do after he left here tonight? Since school was starting tomorrow, there weren't any parties worth going to. And the alcohol had done nothing to quell his libido, which perpetually ran in overdrive anyway.

One of the students at his table was saying something to him, so he forced his attention back to the group. "What?"

A.J.'s smirk was devilish. "I said, we've come up with a wager I think you're going to like."

Despite the mind-deadening effect of the alcohol, Greg's eyes glittered. "Did you say wager?" That was all it took. The spark was lit.

Greg was a man who could never walk away from a bet, however large or small, however outlandish. It was the adventure, the thrill, the fun of it all. He simply could not deny himself. Of course, that was why he now owed his bookie several thousand smackers, plus a few other debts here and there and everywhere. And since on occasion these three students went to the track with him, they were well aware of his unfortunate financial state.

"Now," A.J. said, rubbing his hands together. "You find this Hole-in-the-Sky Mine you were bragging about in class and you'll be off the hook to that sleazy little mole you place bets with, and in addition you'll have a few thousand to play around with at the track." He leaned back with a smug look. "Ten big ones, Dr. Fisher."

Greg's empty mug hit the table with a hollow thud. "Ten thousand!" The look he gave the three students across from him was nothing short of incredulous. "You're talking ten *K*?"

The young men nodded.

"You're not joking?"

A.J. shook his head.

Greg narrowed his gaze on the boys, then poured another glass of beer and sat back to nurse it. He turned to Al. "How in Pandemonium did we end up in the Ivy League with all these rich little snots?"

The three students laughed and A.J. remained their chief spokesman. "We rich little snots will also pay your airfare to Colorado. Sound good?"

Greg withheld comment. He wasn't at all sure about this deal. He had to mull it over for a minute or two.

Al patted him on the back and chuckled. "You made the mistake of saying you had nothing to do for the summer. Remember?"

Greg took a big swig of beer and snorted. "I did, didn't I? But can't we find some game to play around here instead? I'm not the mountain-climbing type."

A.J. shook his head. "That's the bet. Take it or leave it."

Greg thought for a minute about all that money, all those crisp new greenbacks lying in the palm of his hand. He nodded slowly. "All right, I'll take it. I just damn sure will. But you reckless neophyte tycoons might as well go on and start writing out the check from Daddy's bank account. Lost mine, hah!''

"You might not win, you know."

"You must be kidding. I can find anything."

The students rolled their eyes at each other. "So we've heard. But there is a time limit."

"Yeah? How long?"

"Fifteen days."

Greg's mug was halfway to his mouth when his hand stopped. Fifteen days. A flicker of doubt darted across his mind, but he hoisted the mug and quickly drank the uncertainties away. The alcohol was beginning to take its toll and his perceptions were growing fuzzy around the edges. Suddenly, nothing that was said made much sense. Fifteen days...fifteen days for what? What in blue blazes were they blabbering about? He stubbed out his cigarette and took another drink to help clear his thoughts. It didn't help much. Finally he latched onto some key words: money, mine, money, Colorado, money...oh, yeah, some lost mine. He sat back with a chuckle. "No problem," he boasted to the others. "I can find anything."

"And if you don't?"

He was concentrating on the pool of condensation that had formed around his mug and the thought didn't connect for a second or two. "If you're expecting ten grand from me, forget it. I'm just a professor, remember?"

"That's not what we want," they said.

He studied their faces, trying hard to keep them in focus. "So what do you want?"

"We want in the Vanguard program."

He sniffed derisively. "So do about two hundred other students. You have to be selected."

"Look, Dr. Fisher, you know we've got the grades. We're ripe for it, but the damn thing is so political that we probably don't stand a chance on grades alone. You're on the committee and they'll listen to you. If you gave them our names, they wouldn't turn you down."

Too much beer had flowed this night for him to make a rational decision on anything. But shoot, it didn't matter anyway. He was going to find this crazy mine and get the ten thousand dollars, so he didn't even need to worry about the Vanguard. He hadn't made his list of students for that highly sought-after honor yet. These guys might or might not be on that list. He just didn't want to think about it right now.

"You've got fifteen days, professor. Fifteen days to get some tangible proof that you found it."

"Yeah, yeah." Greg's attention had already swerved back to the tall, dark-haired girl at the other table. He remembered now that she had sat in the back row of his class. She was always attentive, always quick with a provocative question or an incisive comment. He couldn't remember her name though. Sarah, Sally...Sandra...He just couldn't remember. She was wearing a camisole, the tight kind that well-built girls wore around campus. It was pink and made of some kind of knit. It looked nice. Real nice.

He was vaguely aware that he was responding to Al and the students at the table, but he didn't have the vaguest idea what the conversation was about or what he was saying, and only a minute later, it seemed, they had all dispersed and Greg found himself standing at the girl's table, leaning down toward that pale upturned face.

THE SUNLIGHT WAS BURNING its way through the window at just the right angle to land on Greg's side of the bed. He rolled over to shut out the brilliant light, but lying on his side made his head throb. He threw back the covers and let his feet drop to the floor, but that made him queasy. He stood up, but immediately dropped back to the bed. It took him ten minutes to get into the glaring white-tiled bathroom and then he stood for another five minutes staring at the unrecognizable zombie in the mirror.

"Fisher," he mumbled, his tongue as thick as a wad of cotton, "you've got to do something about yourself. You're a wreck."

Was he really as old as he looked right now? He was only thirty-six, but either his birth certificate or the face in the mirror was lying. He was no fool; he was going to go with the birth certificate.

What was it that girl at the bar had said last night? Had she called him irresistible? He squinted at the mirror, hoping it would improve the image. It did; he couldn't see himself nearly as well. Yeah, that was better. Maybe her eyes were all squinched up like that when she said it. Either that or she was totally insane.

He paused, frowning as a terrifying thought came to him. He had asked her out. Was that for tonight? Or when? Sandra, yeah, that was her name. Sandra—he had been right about that anyway. But she said she had never been in any of his classes. He had been so sure of that, positive she had sat in the back row. But then the faces had all started running together like a chalk drawing left out in the rain.

Greg leaned over the sink and brushed his teeth, then shaved and took a quick shower. After he had pulled on a pair of jeans, he went into the kitchen to fix something to eat.

But he couldn't shake off an unsettling feeling. He frowned as fragments of the previous evening came back to him. Bits and pieces of a conversation with A. J. Bertram that he couldn't fit together. His head was too fuzzy to think straight, so he poured a tall glass of orange juice and dialed Al's number.

"Tell me I didn't do what I think I did last night."

Al's chuckle was filled with exhaustion. "I assume you are referring to the bet."

Greg leaned against the papered wall and sipped his cold juice. He had to drink it slowly because the acid felt as if it was burning a hole through his stomach. "Exactly what did I bet?" he croaked.

"That you could find some lost mine within fifteen days and collect ten thousand from A.J. and

the boys. Or, if not, you'd get them into the Vanguard program."

"I didn't."

"You did."

"God!"

"Pray, if you like, but I'd suggest you get started.
They were generous in allowing you a couple of
extra days for your return trip from God-knows-
where, but today definitely counts as day number
one."

"Oh, hey, they probably don't even remember
it...don't you think?...Maybe?"

"Those guys? You must be joking. They haven't
forgotten. And don't expect them to let you forget
it, either. Besides, how else are you going to get that
dough to pay off your bad debts?"

Greg yawned and rubbed his stomach. "I've been
wondering that myself. The bank hinted that I
wouldn't find it as easy to get a loan the next time."

"You're a lousy credit risk. Who could blame
them?"

Greg was silent for a moment. "Well, hell, you
know this contest—or whatever it is—is nothing
more than a mindless little treasure hunt."

"Right."

"A child's game."

"Right."

"I mean, look, all I've got to do is research it a
bit and get some good maps and—"

Al laughed. "Listen, Greg, I'd love to talk about
this for hours. But I've got a class to teach this
morning. And if you plan on calling to enlist my

help, forget it. My phone's going to be off the hook for the next couple of weeks.''

''You're a great pal.''

''Friendship can only go so far. Now, you have loads of fun. And don't fall in any mine shaft. I'll see you soon.''

Fifteen days. Just over two weeks to find something that had never been found by anyone else. The Hole-in-the-Sky Mine. A place so remote that many historians deny its existence. Fifteen days, and on Day One he had a rotten hangover, a girl with no last name expecting him to take her out that night and an ulcer that was beginning to flare up again.

He never had liked summer.

Chapter Two

Anne arranged the loose sprigs of wildflowers in an empty mug and set the colorful bouquet on the metal table outside her tiny green sheepherder's trailer. It was an inherently feminine action and she scoffed at herself for succumbing to it. Such a silly girlish thing to do. Normally she resisted the urge to pick the flowers from the meadows, as she resisted most urges that other women found completely natural. But there were times like today when the sun, the air, the waving grasses, and all the blues and yellows and red and pinks of the fields conspired together to form a longing for so many things that she had chosen to give up.

She had picked up her mail at the ranger station a few miles away and over the next ridge, and now sifted through it, finding a letter from her mother. She heated some tea in the metal pot on the camp stove and, feeling a pang of hunger, grabbed an apple from a box the forest ranger had given her. She settled herself comfortably in the hammock that was strung between two trees, the letter resting on her lap, and listened to the sound of the water in a nearby stream as it tumbled over the rocks and splashed onto the thick green banks, saturating the tiny grasses that bordered it. After a while she picked up the letter and began to read.

As with all of Ruth Holdenfield's letters, this one literally bubbled over with family news. Aunt Bess had just turned seventy-five and had insisted once again on a bacchanalian blowout to celebrate the passing of another year. Arthur Holdenfield, Anne's father, was busy writing his essays on the American spirit and on individual freedom. Anne laughed to herself. Good old Dad, reaching for immortality through the written word. Her mother had intimated in a previous letter that this "Emersonian phase" of Arthur's was a sore point between them. After all, weren't there enough fix-ups around the old house to keep him busy so he didn't have to hibernate in the study all day? After so many years of working in academia, he had retired and she finally had him all to herself. She wasn't about to let him shut her out of his life for one more day.

Old habits are awfully hard to break, Mother, Anne thought to herself. As she so well knew.

She swatted away a mosquito that had landed on her leg and lay still as a cool afternoon breeze rustled the pine needles above her and wafted across her face and arms. It was a purely sensuous moment and this time she didn't even stop to deny herself the pleasure. After several delicious minutes, she held up the letter and continued to read.

Once all of the family activities had been described in the minutest of details, there were the inevitable mother-daughter questions, which Anne did her best to silently answer.

When was she coming home for a visit?

Maybe in the fall, Mother, I don't know. I've given up personal commitments, remember?

How was the research going?

Wonderful. Better than could be expected, actually. She had catalogued several new varieties of plants this summer and the elk and deer had been grazing in the valleys nearby.

Did the university plan to extend the grant for another year?

Who could tell what they would do? She certainly hoped so, though. What on earth would she do with herself if she had to face a classroom every day instead of this?

Had she heard from that nice young man she brought home at Christmas?

No, Mother, that relationship, like all of my previous ones, did not work out. James Overland was his name. Whatever it had been between them had lasted exactly six weeks—and a passionless, colorless relationship all the way. Or if a color could be applied in that case, it would have to have been black.

They had met at a university function, a social get-together for all the doctoral candidates in the biology department. Anne had been there and, unfortunately, so had James Overland. Why he had picked her out of the crowd she would never know, but he did and it was she whom he chose to nurse him through some mysterious emotional trauma in his life. As if she didn't have enough of her own problems, she had taken on his, too. And too late she had learned that she was standing in for a wife who had grown tired of him and wanted a midyear fling of her own.

Disaster upon disaster her life with men seemed to be. First it was her marriage to Frank, which though it had a cordial ending still had a definite end to it. And then there was the graduate math student who liked her for only one reason—and it certainly wasn't her mind. Then there was Bernard, who turned out to be gay. And then this fiasco with a married man.

She certainly knew how to pick them! And so she had decided that the best path for her was the solitary one, the one leading to total noninvolvement. She was just glad that she was up here all alone, with no one to bother her, and that she could concentrate on what was important in her life—her work. Just her and the flowers and the animals and the blue sky. Nothing to put a strain on her emotions. Nothing calling for her to use her heart. Safe and uninvolved.

"I worry about you, dear."

Anne let the letter fall to her lap and leaned back against the hammock, one arm shading her eyes from the sun. *I know you do, Mother. So do I.*

Later Anne carefully folded up the letter and slipped it back into the envelope, and a swift spasm of loneliness surged through her for the first time in a long, long time. Next month she would hike back over to the ranger station and leave a letter to be mailed to her mother. Something cheery and full of bright news. She would tell her about her work, about Solomon—the lone ram she had spotted, about the green of the valleys and the lavender and rose and lemon and blue of the flowers that covered the mountain slopes, about the creek that bubbled along near her campsite, washing over the slick granite boulders as it hurried toward the large rivers below. And maybe she would promise to come home in the fall. She had to admit it would be nice to see her parents again and to observe the lasting contentment they had found with each other.

Anne gazed up at the clear blue sky showing through tree branches that filled the air with the scent of pine. Observations. They had become her way of life.

GREG'S RESEARCH was not going well. In fact, after all the digging and drilling, he had hit a very dry hole. There was only a smattering of information about the Hole-in-the-Sky Mine in western Colorado or about Pervis "Stoneface" Johnson, the prospector who had discovered its vein, panned and sifted its wealth, and propagated its mysteries. Surely once he got to Colorado he would find more in the libraries there. He certainly hoped so. Otherwise he was going to be out of ten grand and into a heap of trouble with the university for playing favorites with three overly indulged graduate students.

He had at least obtained the name of a man who might be willing to guide him up into the mountains to look for this legendary mine. Willard Hopkins was his name, a self-proclaimed naturalist, wilderness expert and mountain climber. Greg didn't really care what the guy chose to call himself, as long as he could take him where he wanted to go and ultimately help him win the bet.

He closed the thick book he had been reading and leaned back in his chair, wishing he could have a cigarette. He twirled a pencil between his fingers as a poor substitute. He checked his watch. Five hours and ten minutes he had been here in the university library trying to piece together the story behind the mine. He knew there had to be more, especially as far as some educated guesses as to its exact location, but he just hadn't come across them yet. He had to keep digging. Day One was almost gone.

Greg pulled another book over and opened it. How did he get into these sticky messes anyway? First the bookie, then this harebrained bet with his students. He had been told—numerous times to be truthful—that he needed to grow up. But doggone it, he wasn't ready. He never had been, and maybe he never would be. That was why he went into teaching in the first place, because he hadn't been ready to leave college. He liked being around all those carefree students—especially the women. He liked being around all that young naïveté. They were so easy to influence and mold; he didn't even have to work that hard at it. They just sort of flocked to him, hovered on his every word, eagerly soaking up whatever essence it was that he emitted. He never figured out exactly where his charm lay, but he wasn't going to waste too much time trying to analyze it, either. Wherever it came from, Greg was just very glad it was there.

It was an article about the Rocky Mountain passes in the West Elk range that held his concentration when he realized he was not alone at the table. When he raised his head, the girl, who had been standing on the other side of the table, sat down in a chair and smiled sweetly at him. The first two buttons of her blue blouse were unfastened and a St. Christopher medal nestled in an abundance of cleavage. Her brown hair was streaked with summer-blond strands, and her lips and eyes were all soft and dewy.

"Excuse me for bothering you, Dr. Fisher," she said in a soft, sexy voice. "I wouldn't want to do anything to...like, get in your way or anything."

She rested her arms on the table and leaned forward, giving a clear view of the merchandise. With tremendous willpower Greg forced his eyes to remain glued on her face. "No problem." He cleared his throat and tried again. "No problem."

"I just...well, gee, I just wanted to tell you how really awesome it would be if I could get into your Colonial America class next year. The problem is it's for seniors only unless you get special permission. And, well, I mean, like, I would do anything…*anything* at all…to be in that class…with you.'' She looked down with just the appropriate touch of shyness, and Greg came to the immediate, blood-pounding conclusion that he would kill to have her in his class. Not just in his class, but in his bed. Today. This afternoon. Now.

He started to slam the reference book closed and suggest that very intriguing idea, but a rude spike of sanity thrust itself through him. It was the calendar that was lying open in front of him that did it. June eleventh. Day One.

He smiled bravely at the girl across from him and tried to convince himself that he was doing the right thing. ''Why don't you write down your name….'' And address and phone number, he wanted to add, but refrained from asking. ''And I'll see what I can do about getting you the permission you need.''

She gave a huge sigh. ''Oh, thank you, Dr. Fisher. Thank you so so much. I mean that would just be soooo awesome. If there's anything you want…like, anything at all…''

He cleared his throat when he noticed a couple of students at the next table giggling over the exchange, and patted her hand. ''It's no problem, really. Now, I think I had better get back to my research.''

Disappointed over the brush-off but remaining stoic all the same, the girl hastily wrote her name on a piece of notebook paper and handed it to him. She stood up to go and, with one last coy smile, sashayed her way out of the library and out of his life—at least for the next fourteen days.

With one last longing glance in her direction, Greg sighed and went back to the mountain of maps and periodicals and books that towered on the table in front of him.

ANNE SHIVERED inside her gray rain slicker as she crept through a patch of tall fir, being especially careful not to snap any of the dry twigs that had fallen to the ground. The thick ground cover of needles and bark and kinnikinnick was slick under the soles of her boots. The rain was still falling steadily, but it was not a heavy rain, just one that would continue to fall for several more hours. And up this high it was very cold, the gray clouds hanging well below the tops of the mountains, drifting in and out of the trees around her.

Anne came out of the forest and climbed up onto a gnarled promontory, staying down low and close to the wet rocks so she would not be seen. The shelf ran about forty feet and then hollowed out into a smooth saddle. The rocks were slick from the rain, and she nearly lost her balance several times, but she kept going. She wasn't going to lose Solomon. She had picked up his trail for two days now and had been following him for hours on end. She felt drawn to discover something. Something new and wondrous. His behavior was an enigma to her, and she convinced herself that it was solely of biological importance, a puzzle that the scientist in her had to solve.

He still had not joined up with the other rams. He was alone, traversing the mountainside on a mission of his own. He foraged for grass and herbs, eating the tiny buds and shoots off the newly sprouting trees, then moved to a new and higher grassy bench among the craggy rocks. Anne tried to stay above him or at least at equal level to him, while still maintaining her cover in the protected gullies and rock slides.

The ewes were off summering with the young sheep, and the older males had banded together, leaving the females to have their lambs. An expectant ewe would slip away from the band and climb to a sheltered ledge to bear her young. It was a fairly rigid pattern of behavior, and last summer Anne had spent most of her time with the females. But this summer she had planned to watch the rams, to see where they went and observe their every move. And she still planned to, but this one lone sheep was an intriguing diversion. He had moved into a new territory, away from all that was familiar, away from the patterns that had been set for him. If he was searching for something, he didn't seem to know where to begin looking. If he was lost, he did not appear to be afraid because of it. Why was this ram different from all the rest? Where was he going and what was he seeking?

Anne didn't know, but she would follow his lead. Something stronger than her will told her she could do no less. An opportunity like this comes along once in a lifetime. The chance to find something new and different, something unpredictable and fresh. She had given up looking for the unique in her own life, but she could at least find it in her work.

She huddled inside her slicker and slid along the bluff, following the trail of the ram.

IT WAS RAINING when Greg landed in Gunnison, Colorado, a gloomy overcast day that did not bode well for his introduction into this foreign land. He was a city boy. Though his father had been a military man and the family had moved from place to place until Greg went off to college, he still considered himself city born and bred. He was not the mountain type, he felt sure. The fact that he couldn't even catch his breath at eight thousand feet told him that. He peered up at the snow-tipped lofts that were waiting, like sleeping dragons, for him to make one false step, and once again he wondered what he had gotten himself into.

Bottom line, Greg old boy. You need the bread. So here you are. Fatalistically resigned to the task at hand, he looked for a motel. It was June and the tourist season had begun, but he was able to find an adequate room for the night. That was all he needed anyway. Tomorrow he was heading for tent city. *Fisher,* he told himself, *you're going to be a mountain man.*

By four-thirty that afternoon he had been to the Western State college library in Gunnison to fill in the gaps in his research, to the Forest Service office for maps and to a sporting goods store for needed supplies. He was now entering the Cattlemen's Steak House, where he was to meet his guide into the untrammeled wilderness.

A man sitting by himself at a table signaled to him and Greg walked over.

"Willard Hopkins?"

"Yep. You must be Fisher."

Greg sat down, ordered a beer and lit a cigarette. Willard was just polishing off the beer he had in front of him. He was older than Greg had expected, close to sixty maybe, with gray hair, a flattened boxer's nose and a face that was furrowed with the deep grooves and ravines of hard and fast living. He wore faded denims, a down vest over a plaid cotton shirt and a pair of silver-colored cowboy boots that smelled of horse. A cowboy hat rested on a nearby empty table.

"Yep," the man said. "When I seen you walk through the door, I says to myself, Willard, that there's your Easterner."

Greg chuckled. "That obvious, huh?" The waitress set a full mug down in front of him and he took a grateful drink. Willard ordered another for himself.

"'Fraid so."

"This is my first time here. It's an...interesting state."

"God's country. It's as close to heaven as I'll ever get. How 'bout you?"

Greg took a quick fortifying drink. Heaven? If this was heaven, he was in bigger trouble than he thought. "Yeah, sure," he mumbled noncommittally.

Willard nodded slowly. "So, you ready?"

"I went up to the college library this morning," Greg said. "I was trying to find some more information. But there isn't much to be found, is there?"

"Nope, not much. It's gonna be like looking for a needle in a haystack."

"What can you tell me about the mine and this man Johnson?"

"Pervis Johnson?"

"Yeah, the prospector who found the mine."

Willard leaned back in his chair. "People 'round here just called him Stoneface. Fit his disposition was the way I heard it. Well, let's see, he came from back East somewheres. Some folks claimed he was a doctor who had lost his license. I don't think anyone knew for sure."

"That was in 1880 that he came here, wasn't it?"

"Well, you may be right, son. To tell you the truth, the only date I remember is my own birth date. March 16...no, 17, 192...well, never mind. But you're probably right. Anyway, he came out here and took hisself a Ute squaw, then headed up into the high country in search of gold."

"I've been studying the maps, Mr. Hopkins, and I've got it narrowed down to two or three possible locations."

"Call me Willard, son. The tax assessor and the preacher call me Mr. Hopkins. And neither of them is welcome in my house."

Greg nodded to the older man. "Okay." He pulled out one of the maps and spread it out on the table between them. "Anyway, Willard, I think it must be in here...somewhere."

Willard looked the map over. "Could be right. But, ya know, a lot of folk have been up there looking for that old lost mine. Nobody's had any luck yet. It's just too damn high, too many tricky ridges and canyons. There's parts of this range that ain't never been crossed, 'cepting maybe by Injuns."

"I understand what you're saying, Willard. But maybe no one has ever wanted to find it as badly as I do."

"What fer?"

"Uh...well, it's important to me." *Okay, Fisher, you turkey, you jumped into this hole. Now get yourself out of it.* "You see, I'm a history professor and...well, I've been very interested in this whole area for a long time. I even teach a class called Stampede of the West. It's all about the nineteenth century in the Rockies, the call of the frontier, gold fever, the demise of Indian territory." *Nice touch, Greg. Keep it up.* "It's one of the more popular classes. American kids are just naturally fascinated by tales of the Wild West."

Willard's eyes were trained on Greg's face. He hadn't swallowed one bit of that collegiate hogwash. But to Greg's relief, the man didn't pursue it. "Well," Willard said, "maybe you'll find her, then, and you'll have sumpthin' new to tell your classes. But it ain't gonna be easy. It's gonna be rough going and up so high you'll feel like your lungs are popping out.'' He smiled broadly. ''But danged it's sumpthin' up there. I sure wish I could go along.''

Greg slowly stubbed out his cigarette in the ashtray. His eyes were fixed on the older man and it took a couple of seconds for the statement to filter all the way through his brain. ''What do you mean, *wish* you could go along?'' He laughed nervously. ''You're my guide.''

Willard wiped his mouth with the back of his hand. ''Didn't I tell you? Doggone, I could've sworn I told ya. I can't go.''

''You can't go! Why not?''

''My son-in-law is in the hospital over in Grand Junction and my daughter's coming to get me day after tomorrow to take me over there. Kinda wants me with her, I guess.''

He was going to stay calm. He really was. ''I don't know these mountains, Willard. Hell, what am I saying, I don't know any mountains. I can't go by myself.''

''Wish I could go, son. I surely do. But...well, this other thing just popped up like that...gallstones I think my Lucy told me it was. Anyways, I just gotta go over there.''

Greg took a huge drink of his beer, recalculating the time left. This was Day Two. Okay, no problem. He just had to think it all through, that was all. He had made it this far, no backing out now. He reached down and pulled a stack of papers from his satchel. ''Here,'' he said, pulling one out and setting it in front of him. ''Here is the list of guides I have. You were the first on the list, that's why I called you. But maybe I could get one of these others."

"Lemme see that," Willard said, taking the paper and holding it up close to his eyes. He pulled a short, fat pencil from his vest and marked through the first couple of names. "These two ain't even here anymore." He marked through another one. "Nah, you don't want this clown. He doesn't know his butt from apple butter." He moved to the next. "This one's already up in the Sawatch with some people. And this one's up Cochetopa. No, you don't want this 'un. Now this feller's dead and buried over at Marble." He handed the list back to Greg. "That's it, son, there ain't none left."

"Surely there's someone who could lead me up there. I'm willing to pay a fair amount."

"I knowed you are. But there's none that I'd let lead me crost the street. The best ones are already tied up for the summer. Now, if you could wait a few days for me to get back—"

"No!" Greg quickly tried to soften his tone. "I can't do that. I need to keep to my schedule."

"Okay," Willard said, watching him closely. "Tell you what. I feel right bad about this, so here's what I'm gonna do, son. In the morning, I'm gonna drive you up Ohio Creek and up Mill Creek Road a piece. It's not the direction I would have started us, but at least from there you can walk a couple or three miles or so up to Anne Holdenfield's patch."

"Who's Anne Holdenfield?"

"She's this lady scientist or sumpthin' or nuther that lives her summers up in an old Basque sheepherder's trailer. She studies the bighorn up there above timberline, follows 'em around. She might could help ya."

"How can some crazy broad who trails around after sheep help me?"

"'Cause she knows that area better'n just about anybody. She's been living up there for the past four summers, traipsing all over them rocks. She knows it all right. Better'n anybody."

With Willard's help, Greg found Mill Creek Road on the map in front of him. That was south of where he wanted to start, but if this woman were to help him…"And you think she would lead me to the area where I think the mine could be?"

Willard shrugged. "Maybe. Maybe not. There ain't much telling what that gal'll do. She's an odd bird, she is. And she may just turn her shotgun on you. But it can't hurt to try, now can it?"

"That depends on if she shoots first and asks questions later," Greg mumbled.

Willard got a big kick out of that one. "Heck fire," he said with a laugh, "an Eastern city slicker like you ought to be able to charm the claws right off a female grizzly. That Holdenfield gal shouldn't pose no problem 'tall. No sirree, not 'tall."

Chapter Three

It was bright and early the next morning when Greg emerged from his motel room, all decked out in the new L. L. Bean clothes he had hurriedly bought the day before coming to Colorado. Willard Hopkins was waiting for him in his World War II vintage jeep, a beer can clutched in one hand and the wrist of his other hand dangling over the steering wheel.

"Godamighty, son! You look like you jest stepped out of the pages of one of them magazines. You gonna climb around in them duds?"

Greg laughed and looked down at his clothes. "I told you, I've never been to the mountains before. I didn't know what to bring. The salesman in the store insisted that this was what everyone wore out here."

Willard glanced down at his own clothes. He was wearing the same thing he had worn the day before. "Guess I'm sorta behind the times then," he said, brushing at a speck of dirt in his shirt. "Hop on in and let's get movin'."

Greg climbed in and sat down on the dust-covered seat. He had thought about this adventure quite a bit during the night, and he had come to the conclusion that Willard was right. He could charm anyone into doing just about anything he wanted. He'd always been able to. Especially women. For some reason, all he had to do was give them a soulful look and they just seemed to melt. it was something he had that worked. So he had decided during the night that even if Willard couldn't guide him, he would surely be able to talk this shepherdess into it. After all, women were basically all alike. Yes, everything was going to work out just fine. As Willard had put it, no problem 'tall.

He was in high spirits this morning as Willard drove through the small town of Gunnison and then turned off the highway onto Ohio Creek Road toward the West Elk Mountains. The air was piercingly sweet, the night's rain having left everything fresh and new. The road serpentined through a lush green valley, much of it privately owned ranches, where scrubby pine and sage bordered fields brilliant with the colors of wildflowers. Mixed with wild rye and foxtail barley were the reds and yellows of Indian paintbrush, goldenrods, asters and thistles.

"From what I've read," Greg said, "this valley was among the important ones during the mining days."

"Yep. There was a lot of coal mining up in this area. Baldwin, Castleton, lots o' little towns sprung up."

"That's the strange thing about this mine I'm looking for. This was coal country around here, wasn't it? Yet Pervis Johnson claimed he had a gold mine."

"I know what you mean," Willard agreed. "Up in Taylor Park there was lots of gold. But here...." He shook his head. "Not too much of it around here 'cept for old Stoneface's Hole up there."

Greg studied the rise of mountains to the west and north. "The facts back up his claims. It definitely was gold."

Willard nodded slowly. "These mountains hold a mess of secrets, son. A whole mess of 'em."

After a while they turned off Ohio Creek. "This is Mill Creek Road. I'll take ya up it a piece, but it's rough going and the road don't go too far. You'll have to start walking in a little while."

Willard was right about the road. It was very rough going. It was washed out in some spots and he maneuvered the jeep across it with the finesse of a tank in a mine field. It sloped gradually upward for a couple of miles and then began a steeper climb as it rose up into the range of mountains. The morning air was crystal clear and every sound seemed magnified in the thin, dry air.

After a couple of hours Willard pulled the jeep to a halt on the dirt road. "Here you go."

Greg gazed around at the towering landscape, at the field of wildflowers to his right and the steep grassy rise to his left. A thin trail led up at an angle, then disappeared in the stand of trees at the top of the slope. "Here? This?"

"Yep, this is the place. See, all you got to do is follow this trail for a mile or so. After you get through that first thicket it'll open up into a meadow. The path'll fork there. You take the one to the left. That'll be straight west. Follow it for another half mile and then you'll reach a small clearing. Her trailer'll be there."

If Willard recognized panic in Greg's white-faced, tight-lipped expression, he made no comment. To him, it was as simple as following a little path. To Greg, it was a walk through the Twilight Zone.

"What if I get lost?"

Willard snorted. "You ain't gonna get lost, son. Jest follow the danged trail."

"You're sure the path is clearly marked?"

Willard rubbed his chin. "Well, it was last summer. Could be washed out a bit now. Yep, could be. But Hector's puppy dogs, you'll be able to pick it up again. You're gonna be going north a bit, then west, then northwest, then west. You got your compass?"

Greg pulled it from his jeans pocket and checked the direction. "Let's see, we're now facing—"

"You've got it upside down, boy."

"Oh." Greg corrected the position. "Okay, we're facing north...."

"Northeast. Lordamighty, son, don't you know how to read a compass?"

Greg crammed it back into his pocket and grabbed his pack from the back of the jeep. "I just read it, didn't I?"

"Don't go getting surly on me, now." Willard chuckled and wiped a sleeve across his mouth. "You're gonna be fine and dandy. You jest follow that path like I told ya, and you'll find that Holdenfield gal's trailer." He laughed again, and this time the sound was like a whistle through his teeth. "And boy, you'd better start practicin' the charm. You've got a heckuva job ahead of you."

Greg scowled at the older man as he slipped on the heavy pack and adjusted the strap around his waist. He had everything Willard insisted he would need: his bedroll, a thin nylon tent, some packets of food and dried meats, matches in a waterproof container, a flashlight, a first-aid kit, a thin reflective blanket, a canteen of water and a couple of fresh changes of clothes. He had also added a few extras—a camera, some Milky Way bars, a carton of cigarettes and a flask of bourbon—his own personal list of the necessities of life.

Greg hadn't pumped iron since high school gym class, but he was positive that it had never been as tough as what he was now doing. He was miserable. The straps of the pack cut into his shoulders and he felt that if he didn't stoop forward, he would surely fall backward down the mountain.

He pulled his pack of cigarettes from his shirt pocket and struck a match on the side of the jeep. "Well..." He lit the tip of the cigarette and inhaled deeply. "I appreciate you bringing me up here, Willard."

"Wish I could go with you, boy. I can tell it would be a real hoot."

Greg glanced at the old man to try and read what he meant by that, but Willard was in the process of picking his teeth with a pocket knife and was gazing across the field of flowers.

Greg surveyed the wild land around him and took a deep drag on his cigarette. "Okay, well...guess I'll see you when I get back to town."

"Yep."

He stood on the side of the road and watched Willard back the jeep around. With one final wave, the old man headed back down the road toward Ohio Creek, and from there back to civilization. Greg watched until the jeep disappeared in its own dust around the next curve in the road.

He stubbed out his cigarette with the toe of his hiking boot. Just that simple act made him realize something else. He had bought the wrong shoes. Or the wrong size or something. His feet were killing him. He couldn't even feel three of the toes on his left foot. They were completely numb.

Fisher, what in hell are you doing here? You're getting too old for this. Hitching the pack up higher on his shoulders, he turned and faced the mountain. "Okay," he said, nodding to the terrain. "Okay, so you're big and steep and all that. So what? Hey, I saw *Jeremiah Johnson*. Three times in fact. If Robert Redford can do it, I certainly can. No problem."

He took a couple of steps up the incline, then stopped. By stretching his arm back he was just able to reach the side pocket of his pack. He unzipped it and pulled out a king-size Milky Way, then tore off the wrapper and dropped it to the ground.

The candy bar was devoured before he reached the top of the first hill. At the crest he looked down at the road that snaked below him. A creek ran alongside it, flowing beneath the willow bushes that grew against its banks. The path ahead of him was still on the incline as it headed up into the thick grove of pine and fir and spruce.

The pack was heavy on his back, but he was getting used to it. The air was cooler in the shade, and he stopped to rest on fallen trees every few minutes to catch his breath. He was convinced now that he should have gone into training for this. If he had known what it was going to be like he would have told those three students of his to take a flying leap.

A chipmunk dashed down the trunk of the pine Greg was sitting beneath and scampered across a fallen log to hide under a rock. A stellar jay screeched out a warning and then flew off to the top of a tree.

Greg pulled out his canteen for a long drink. He lit another cigarette and sat quietly smoking. He had been hiking now for almost an hour and he had no idea how far he had come. Maybe a mile, maybe not even that far. Willard had said the path came out into a meadow after a mile, but he didn't see any sign of a meadow yet.

If his feet didn't hurt so bad he might find something humorous about all of this. Here he was, sitting on a log in the middle of nowhere, and it was really the first time he had thought about why he was here. Oh, he had considered it on the more superficial level. He had been drunk and made a bet with his students. He needed the money. He loved a challenge. He had been bored with the summer already. But was that all it was? Boredom, money, adventure. Not bad reasons for flying twenty-five hundred miles and trekking through the Rocky Mountain wilderness on his own, he decided.

Things had always come easily for him, and he certainly wasn't going to complain about that. School had been easy—so easy, in fact, that he decided to stay in rather than get out and face the more real, more adult world. He liked the sure paths, the easy conquests, the tangible rewards. He didn't want to have to work too hard for anything. He preferred to play. Wine, women and song was his favorite tune. He was a hedonist and damn proud of it.

So why was he here? This certainly wasn't fun. There was no wine, no women, no songs if you discounted the screech of those obnoxious birds. The biggest thrill of the day had been when he was munching on that Milky Way. Not exactly a hedonist's dream come true.

He expelled a tired breath and stood up, pulling on his pack once again. He might as well stop looking for hidden meanings in this masochistic romp through the wilds. He was here to find the lost mine, that was all. And he certainly wasn't going to find it if he didn't get off his rear and start moving.

After another quarter of an hour he came to the meadow. It was about a mile wide and the trail cut straight across it. A rippling stream angled through the willow thickets, and the whole field was wet and marshy. Marsh marigolds grew in clusters in the moist soil, their white buttercuplike heads glistening in the bright sunlight. His jeans became soaked up to his knees as he waded through the wet brush. At one point something big and brown moved in the dense thicket, but he couldn't tell what it was. He hoped it was just a deer.

He crossed the meadow and headed back up into the dark cover of pine. The path disappeared occasionally or angled off in about three different directions. Deer and elk had made new ones and several times he had to backtrack to pick up the main hiking trail. Worn out from the endeavor, he stopped and pulled his lunch from the pack and sat down by the edge of a stream to eat it. The motel had packed him a couple of ham sandwiches with cheese, some grapes and a plum, and a large Hershey's bar. He ate heartily, finishing up everything in the sack, soaked his tired, aching feet in the stream, then sat back against the bank and smoked with his eyes closed.

The time slipped idly by while Greg quietly absorbed the forest sounds and scents that surrounded him. But soon a loud crack and roll shook the air and he reluctantly opened his eyes. Dark clouds had rolled in and their angry rumble reverberated across the sky. "Well, that's just great," he muttered. "Just great."

He wearily pulled on his miserable, too-tight boots, adjusted the pack on his back and started along the trail once again.

ANNE PROPPED HER FEET up on the cot inside the trailer and read through the day's entry in the journal.

> June 13
> The weather has been good today, except for a brief shower and hailstorm around noon. This morning I took my two cameras up to Edgar's Summit and photographed some marmots and ptarmigans. While lunching I spotted a Clark's nutcracker stealing eggs from the ptarmigan's nest while the female was away feeding.

After lunch I headed over to the Divide where the ram has spent the last two days. He has remained placid, feeding on the buds and shoots of bushes and young trees. He still has not joined up with the rest of the male herd and I am fairly certain that he will not do so.

Tomorrow morning I will pack my gear and go up to watch the herd. I am not leaving the ram, only giving him and myself a bit of space between us. I think he is aware of my presence and I do not want it to affect his behavior. I will pick up his trail again on the day after tomorrow.

Anne closed the spiral notebook and let her boots drop to the floor. She stood up and stretched, then grabbed an empty cup from the shelf and opened the trailer door. The afternoon was sweet with the fresh smell left from the rain. The meadow was in full bloom—Rocky Mountain iris, purple-eyed mariposa, coralroot and primrose nestled in the tall rye and bear grass—and the colors were deep and soft in the hazy afternoon light.

For a good part of every year Anne, like the other animals here, was a creature of this environment. She breathed the thin air and drank the spring waters and knew the peace of having only sheep and marmots and stellar jays as her companions. The fact that she was oftentimes lonely was something she refused to acknowledge, for she believed that the rhythms of her body had become inexorably tied to the rhythms of the alpine eco-system, and no other more human sentiment would be allowed to intrude.

She stepped down from the trailer and walked over to the table where her Coleman stove was sitting. She was just reaching for the coffeepot on the burner when she caught a flash of something in the distance. She raised her head and looked down the slope toward the south edge of the clearing. It was a man. He was standing there, smoking a cigarette and staring up at her camp.

She stared back, not moving, still holding the handle of the coffeepot. Occasionally she had visitors—mostly the noisy intrusion of campers on dirt bikes. But this man appeared tentative, as if he was not at all sure whether he wanted to approach.

When he finally started to walk in her direction, she carefully and inconspicuously picked up her rifle and cradled it across her arms. And she kept her eyes trained on his every move.

IT WAS THREE O'CLOCK in the afternoon before he had come to the final clearing. About fifty yards ahead, nestled back in the edge of the trees, he had seen the trailer. The green, Basque sheep-herder's type, curved at the top like a Conestoga wagon. It was so small he couldn't imagine how anyone—especially a woman—could stand living in it for a whole summer.

The sun had finally come back out but was now almost below the top of the mountains and the light sliced at an angle across the clearing and onto the trailer. All was quiet around it, but a thin trail of smoke rose from an outdoor fire pit. A table was set up in the yard with a camping stove on it, and some jeans and shirts and underwear hung from the pine branches near the fire.

He had been standing there, wondering to himself what kind of lunatic would choose to live like a hermit in the middle of the wilderness, when she came out of her trailer. She had walked to her stove and was now holding a rifle loosely over her arms as he moved closer to the camp.

He reached the tree where her jeans and a dainty lace camisole were hanging to dry, and he stopped, staring first at the delicate underwear hanging before him and then at the woman they belonged to. ''Hello.''

Still holding the gun across her arm, she poured coffee into her cup without responding, yet she watched him closely. The man looked like a wet puppy, standing there with water dripping from his hair, his face sunburned and his lungs struggling for breath. Another of life's desperate, searching for an escape, she decided inhospitably.

She watched his eyes return again to the clothes hanging to dry and she cursed herself for leaving them there. The jeans and shirt she didn't mind, but the lacy underwear was a sure sign of feminine weakness that she did not want to even admit to, let alone advertise. She would just have to rectify the image with a tough stance.

Greg reached into his pocket for another cigarette. It was soaking wet and crumbled between his fingers. He dropped it to the ground.

Her eyes moved very slowly and deliberately from his face to the litter on the ground. He followed her stare to the crumbled cigarette at his feet and sighed, then awkwardly stooped down with the heavy pack on his back and picked up the trash, cramming the crumbled paper and tobacco into his pocket with the compass. The wet tobacco stuck to his fingers, but he wiped them clean on the front of his shirt.

He squinted his eyes into the sun as he studied the woman across the small campsite. Her hair and eyes were almost the same color—a soft autumn brown—and the angles and curves of her face were covered with creamy unlined skin. The top of her head came to about his chest, so she was probably around five-four or five-five. And from what he could see of her figure, it was as nice as her face.

She was younger than he had expected, mid to late twenties maybe, and definitely a woman, though she obviously tried to hide the fact. But the lacy, flesh-colored camisole hanging across the pine branch gave it away. His eyes moved back from the clothes to her face. Yes, despite the jeans and camouflage shirt, the heavy hiking boots, hair pulled back in a ponytail and no makeup, there was no mistaking that she was a woman. A very interesting one at that.

He smiled to himself. A cinch, that's what this was going to be. Willard had been right. He would have no trouble at all charming the claws off this female grizzly. She was a woman, wasn't she? And Greg Fisher had yet to meet a woman who didn't succumb without a whimper to his charms.

"Are you Anne Holdenfield?" he asked.

She took a sip of her coffee before answering, hiding her surprise. "I am."

He tried to smile confidently, but he was still huffing and puffing too hard to have much success. He stepped closer, reaching out to shake her hand. "My name is Greg Fisher."

She kept the rifle cradled in her arms. "Wonderful. I'll alert the media."

He chuckled even though she had not. She hadn't even cracked the teeniest smile. But he forged on ahead. "Looks like you and I are going to be spending the next few days together."

Holding the cup in one hand, she took another drink of her coffee, then set the cup down without the slightest change in her expression. The next sound Greg heard was the loud catch of the rifle's forearm slide handle as she pulled it back.

He looked at the gun and then at her face. *That was a real dumb thing to say, Greg old boy. Real dumb.* There was absolutely no doubt in his mind now that she was the type of woman who would shoot first and ask questions later. He had been right about her after all. Interesting face and body or not, this one was a bona fide nut case.

A trickle of moisture ran down the side of his face. Ten thousand dollars. He had gotten himself into this mess over ten grand. And on Day Three what was he doing? He was standing face-to-face in the wastelands of the world with a raving lunatic.

Chapter Four

Charm. Charm. Where was it? He knew he had it in there somewhere. *Pull it out, Fisher!*

He chuckled lightly. "Surely that's not intended for me." He tried again. "There isn't a bullet in there with my name on it, is there?"

"That all depends."

"On what?"

"On whether you move or not."

A bird fluttered in the tree above him. "I have to move sometime. I can't stay like this forever."

"We'll see about that."

Greg expelled a heavy breath. "Look, lady, I'm bushed. I've been walking most of the day to get here and I'm soaking wet. I just want to sit down, maybe have a cup of your coffee, smoke a cigarette and relax. I'm certainly not here to cause you any harm. I don't have the energy for that."

Anne noticed the fatigue in his blue eyes and in the slope of his broad shoulders. "Sit," she said.

He didn't budge. "Does that mean I can move?"

"Right over there," she pointed. "On that log. Sit."

Not about to trust a woman with a gun, he kept his eyes on her as he stepped gingerly over to the log she had indicated, slipped off his pack and sat down. *Look at that lunatic,* he said to himself as he watched her set the butt of her rifle on the ground and lean it back against the table.

"So," she said, "you are now resting. You have exactly five minutes to do so and then you can be on your way."

He rested his forearm on his thighs and stared at her. What a disagreeable woman! "I didn't realize you owned the Rocky Mountains."

She glared at him. "Four minutes and thirty seconds."

"I didn't walk all this way to have a five-minute rest. I came here to talk to you."

"What for?"

He sniffed derisively. "How nice of you to inquire. I don't suppose you would be inclined to offer me a cup of that coffee, would you?"

She glanced at the pot on the stove and then back at her unwanted guest. After a moment of hesitation she picked up an empty cup and poured hot coffee into it. She set it on the edge of the table, then stepped back and leaned against the trailer. Greg reached out for the cup.

"This is good," he murmured after sipping the coffee and feeling its warmth flow through him. "Thanks." When she didn't respond, he added his own reply. "You're welcome, Greg. Ánytime."

"So," she said, ignoring his sarcastic monologue, "you've come all this way to see me."

He took another sip of coffee. "That's right."

"Why?"

"I need your help."

"First of all, who are you?" she asked, holding her own cup of coffee between her hands to warm them.

"I told you. My name is Greg Fisher."

A light breeze lifted the strands of hair near her face. She brushed them back with her fingers. "That means nothing to me."

"Probably not." He shrugged. "Meant quite a lot to my mother, I suppose."

"Where are you from?"

"Princeton, New Jersey." He waited for the inevitable question, but it didn't come, so he supplied it. "I'm a professor at the university there." He sensed a relaxing in her tough stance, so he dove in headfirst. "I have a Ph.D. in history and I'm here on a kind of...of sabbatical, you might say. I'm looking for a legendary mine that's supposedly up this way. The Hole-in-the-Sky. Are you familiar with it?"

"No."

Not a real talkative sort, is she? He lifted the cup to his lips and studied her over the rim. As small and attractive as she was, she came across as tough as Ma Barker. *She would have made a good pioneer woman,* he finally decided. A little too tough-acting for his tastes and not exactly the type he was used to charming, that was for sure, but he could still give it the old college try.

"What are you really here for?" she asked, her eyes narrowed in suspicion; she felt an uneasiness that she couldn't quite define.

He laughed nervously. "I told you. I'm on a sabbatical. I'm looking for a lost mine."

"Why don't I believe you?"

Greg looked as innocent as he could. "I don't know. I've always been told I had an honest face."

He smiled the famous Greg Fisher smile, the combination of sensual youth and all-knowing man rolled into one neat little package. "What about you?" he asked, positive that she was already captivated by him.

She stared back blankly. "What about me?"

He cleared his throat. "What do you do?"

She narrowed her eyes at him. She wasn't going to fall for this drivel. She had been around men like this many times. Around the block and back. She had learned the hard way to suspect the entire lot of them. And this man looked about as trustworthy as a hungry wolf in wet sheep's clothing.

She regarded him for a long moment, aware that the uneasiness inside her was growing. His hair was a sandy brown and he had probably the bluest eyes she had ever seen. They were clear and open like the sky, with a hint of wildness like the hyacinth that grew at the tops of slender leafless stems in the meadows. He was taller than she and older by a few years, and she realized with a start that he was one of the most attractive men she had ever laid eyes on.

Forcefully she shook the uncharacteristic thoughts from her head. What was the matter with her? Anne Holdenfield didn't react that way to strange men. She was obviously suffering from some sort of high-altitude sickness.

She tried for her more typical cynicism. *He is handsome, Anne, but only if you like that preppy sort of look. I mean, look at him. He's soaking wet and totally out of his element. And yet he is going to try and pull one of those typical male numbers on you.*

She smiled to herself. Well, she had news for this strutting rooster; he had just entered the wrong barnyard.

He tried again. "I mean, are you a teacher, a writer or..." *A hermit? A lunatic?*

"Wildlife ecologist," she reluctantly admitted, not wanting him to know anything at all about her.

"Really?" he said, reaching for polite interest. "Do you teach at some university?"

"No. You want to tell me what it is you want, so I can get back to my work?"

"I told you, I'm up here to find a lost mine."

"So go find it."

"I thought maybe you might help me." He stood up and smiled, but when he saw her eyes move back to the rifle, he sat back down. "My guide had to back out at the last minute and I was told that you know this area better than anybody."

"Is that right?"

He nodded. "That's what I heard."

"Well, you heard right. I do know it better than anybody."

"So, what do you think?" he smiled. "Would you lead me where I want to go?"

She stared at him for a moment and then laughed lightly. She had to admit he made an intriguing picture sitting there with those straight white teeth and blue eyes, wet hair and clothes, so vulnerable and lost and yet so egotistically confident that she would help him.

She shook her head and chuckled again. "No."

He wiped his forearm across his forehead and stared at her. "No?"

"That's what I said, Fisher. No."

"Why not?"

This time her laugh was short and disbelieving. "I don't have time, that's why. I am on a university grant. I have responsibilities. I can't take the time to go traipsing off to some lost mine. I'm here to study the bighorn."

"It would only be a few days," he argued. "Just a few short days."

She noticed a kind of desperation in his voice that didn't quite fit his image. "Why are you so eager to find this mine? What's so important about it?"

"It's...well, it's a historic site. It needs to be found."

"And what are you going to do with it once you've found it? Open it up as a tourist attraction? Put up a McDonald's? Charge admission?"

"I'll write about it. I could ask you the same thing, you know. What do you do with your bighorn?"

"That's different. By understanding animal behavior we can better understand ourselves."

"Oh, hogwash," he muttered. "Preserving history is just as important. Life is a continuum, constantly repeating itself, We learn from our past."

She shook her head. "The answer is still no, Fisher. I just don't have the time."

"I'll pay you," he said. "I'll make it worth your while." Let's see, the students were giving him ten thousand, eight of which were going to pay off the gambling debts. That left two. "I'll give you fifteen hundred dollars," he said.

"What! Are you crazy! Fifteen hundred dollars!" She was staring at him as if he had lost his mind.

"One thousand five hundred, Miss Holdenfield. That's a lot of money for a few days of hiking."

"You're not up here on any sabbatical," she accused, regarding him with a keen look.

He shrugged. "Okay, okay, you win. I have a bet with some colleagues. Ten thousand dollars to be exact, Miss Holdenfield. Ten thousand smackers. And I'd appreciate your cooperation."

He wants your cooperation, Anne. How dare he! How dare he hike up here with his good looks and try to charm you away from your work. He obviously didn't realize that Anne Holdenfield was impervious to male charm. She had to be. She pulled herself up straighter. *Come on, Anne, get rid of this joker.* "Listen, buster," she snapped, as impatient with herself for listening to him as she was with him. "I don't know or care what your game is or how much money you could win, but I think I've made it clear that I'm not interested. 'No' is my answer. You're going to have to find another way to win your stupid bet."

"There is no other way."

"Then that's your problem. Now if you don't mind, I want to start cooking my dinner and then I have some work to do."

Greg nodded slowly and stood up. He set his cup on the table and adjusted his pack on his shoulders. "Sure, no problem," he said. "Just thought I'd ask."

She frowned slightly at the quick acceptance. That was too easy. Something wasn't quite right about this. He didn't look the type to give up that easily.

"Well, good day to you," he said and walked back in the direction from which he had come.

She watched his back and wondered why she didn't trust him. There was something about him that both interested her and aroused her suspicions at the same time.

When he stopped about fifty feet away and dropped his pack, she knew she had been right not to trust him. She stood still and watched in disbelief as he pulled out his tent and his bedroll and started making camp.

Making camp! Right next to hers!

Like hell he was!

She marched down the slope, carelessly trampling the carpet of wildflowers in her path, and stopped directly in front of where he was kneeling over the collapsed tent. "What do you think you're doing?"

He smiled up at her. "Oh, hello again. What am I doing? I'm trying to figure out how to set up this thing."

"No, you're not."

He glanced back at the lump of blue nylon in front of him. "I'm not?"

"You are not going to make camp right here."

"Oh? Why is that?" He looked down at the ground around him. "Am I crushing some arctic tundra or something?"

"My camp is right there," she said, pointing to her trailer.

"Yes, it is," he replied solemnly.

She sighed heavily. "Look, Fisher, there are thousands of acres around here for you to camp on. Why do you have to camp right next to me?"

He smiled. "I like having neighbors."

"Well, I don't."

"Oh, well, gee, I guess one of us is going to be inconvenienced, then."

"Why are you doing this to me?" she cried. "Why are you disrupting my solitude?"

His smile grew even wider. "Because I like you."

"Bull."

"Come on, Miss Holdenfield, it will be fun. We can sit around the campfire together at night and roast marshmallows and tell ghost stories...hey, where are you going?''

He watched with a sly smile as she trudged back up the slope to her campsite, opened the trailer door and climbed in, then slammed the door shut behind her.

She was not going to let this man affect her that way. There was absolutely no excuse for this volatile behavior of hers. But there was just something about him...something frighteningly masculine with which she did not want to deal. Preservation of the heart was the key to survival. She must not forget that.

The sound of the slamming door echoed against the rocky slopes that towered around them and then slowly faded. But the sound of his voice, reverberating through the canyons of her mind, did not fade so quickly.

SELF-PRESERVATION—that was the key. And so, following her normal daily pattern, Anne was up at the crack of dawn the next morning. She was going to climb up the ridge to the north and see if Solomon was still in the same pasture. On the way, she hoped to photograph Seagler's Lake and the patch of dogtooth violets she had been observing since she came here. The object of these photographs was to record seasonal changes in some typical alpine habitats. She had been photographing these same spots once a week and she wanted to take advantage of today's clear weather to get some good shots.

It was a glorious day, with the sunlight just beginning to glow over the tops of the mountains, a sharp chill in the air, ethereal mists rising from the meadow as the sun rose and warmed the earth. The only blotch on this otherwise perfect morning was the sight of that blue nylon tent that sat crookedly on a patch of ground fifty feet away. Instead of an umbrella tent, he had brought along one with a bunch of poles. Three of them were lying on the ground, unused, and a couple of ropes were tied to the trees to hold the tent up.

I hope he froze in his sleep, she thought inhospitably as she donned her own gear and headed up the slope in the opposite direction. *I hope a pika stole his food. I hope a ground squirrel digs a tunnel under his bedroll. I hope...I hope...*

GREG LAY SHIVERING inside his sleeping bag, too cold to get up and move around even though he knew it would warm him up to do so. The ground felt wet beneath him and the moisture had seeped up into the totally inadequate material of his bedroll. He had spent one perfectly miserable night, the worst he could ever remember. The night sounds of the forest had woven his dreams into nightmares and he was awakened at the crack of dawn by the rat-a-tat tapping of a nearby woodpecker.

He had been lying there unmoving for almost thirty minutes—his limbs frozen—watching the goings on at a particular campsite about fifty feet away. The aloof Miss Holdenfield had arisen early and to his acute disappointment was fully dressed when she came out of her trailer. He had hoped to catch a glimpse of the moldable woman beneath that brittle exterior.

He had watched as she heated water for coffee and cooked something that smelled good in a skillet over the camp stove. Then, after cleaning up her utensils, she had packed her gear and headed across the meadow in the opposite direction.

Where was she going, he wondered. And why didn't she just admit defeat and tell him she'd take him wherever he wanted to go? How long was he going to have to wait around here for her to back down?

He shivered once again beneath the down covering. Well, however long it took, he would have to wait it out. She was his only chance to find the mine and win the bet.

THAT AFTERNOON when she returned from her wanderings, the ugly, crooked blue tent was still there. He had straightened it up a little since the morning, but it was still there. Actually Anne heard him long before she came out into the meadow and saw his camp. Probably every animal for five miles had heard him rattling around down there, too, she thought irritably. If she didn't get that pest out of here soon, he was going to scare off all the wildlife in the forest.

She tried to ignore the intruder while she prepared her dinner, but she could hear him whistling and singing off-key. It was some stupid song about a lady from Shanghai who had told him good-bye and stolen his heart in the wake of her lie. Anne wanted to cover her ears and scream to shut out the sound of his voice as he merrily went about with a clumsy attempt to build a fire and fix his dinner.

Normally she liked to sit out for a while at night, enjoying the warmth of the fire and the light from the stars above. But not tonight. Tonight she couldn't wait to shut herself in the trailer and get away from that irritating man's clatter.

The next day was no better. His tent was still there when she awakened early and left with her camera for her day's outing. And he was there when she returned in the late afternoon. She was fixing her dinner over the fire and listening to another off-key ditty of his when she decided she could stand it no longer. She pulled her skillet off the rack and dropped it to the ground. Standing up and wiping her hands on her pants legs, she stalked down the slope to his camp. He was trying unsuccessfully to light a fire in the evening breeze and he looked up and smiled when he saw her standing over him.

"Oh, hello again. Did you come to borrow a cup of sugar?"

Her hands were pressed into her waist and she glared down at his irritatingly handsome face. "Aren't you going to leave here?"

He stood up and propped his boot on a large boulder, looking down into her warm brown eyes that now sparkled with furious little lights. "Not until you agree to lead me to the mine."

Her expression didn't change. She still had the same stony countenance. "And if I do, will you get out of my hair and then I and these mountains can return to peace and quiet?"

"Yes."

"And I'll never ever see you again in my whole life?"

"Never."

She paused, knowing that without a doubt she was going to regret this in the morning. "We'll start tomorrow at daybreak. Be ready."

With that she turned and stomped back to her trailer, climbing the step and slamming the door behind her.

Greg remained standing, staring after her with a smile. He had won. He had broken her down. He was going to win the ten thousand after all. He pursed his lips. Interestingly enough, she had lasted longer than he had expected. There was something to be admired in a woman like that, he supposed. Of course, thank goodness he didn't run across women like her very often. She was, as Willard had said, an odd bird.

Still—there was something to be admired....

Chapter Five

It was the sharp job to the ribs that pulled him out of his deep frozen sleep.

"Ouch! Hey, what the. . ." Greg sat up in the bedroll and stared up at the imposing figure standing at the entrance to his tent. "What did you do that for?"

Anne cocked her head and looked down from her superior position. "It's time to go."

"It's not even morning," he groaned, then noticed the pale pink flush through the trees. "Just barely," he conceded begrudgingly.

Anne tried to conceal a smile. She studied the way his tousled hair fell across his forehead and she had the irrational urge to sweep it back with her fingers, but she successfully restrained herself from doing so. His eyes held a sleepy, dismayed expression and he looked half frozen. Still, she wasn't going to have an ounce of sympathy for him. He presumably got into this of his own free will and if he was out of his element it was his own fault. She wasn't going to take the time or energy to worry about him. All she wanted to do was get him out of there so she could have some solitude once again. If guiding him to this mine would do that, then that's what she would do.

"Get up. We have to get moving."

Greg unzipped his sleeping bag and climbed out, fully dressed. He had on two pairs of socks, jeans, a flannel shirt and his coat.

Anne laughed when she noticed how he was dressed. "You're going about it all wrong. Don't you know that you're supposed to sleep nude in a down sleeping bag?"

"Nude!" He stared at her as if she were insane. "What do you take me for—a complete idiot? I nearly froze as it was."

"But that's the problem," she said. "The clothes are what makes you cold. Down is meant to be worn next to your skin. It insulates your body and keeps the heat in better. Like the Eskimos do." She laughed again and walked over to his fire pit. "Try it tonight and see if it doesn't make a difference."

Greg stood up and began rolling up the bedding and loading his pack. He glared at Anne, who was kicking dirt over the dying embers of his fire and doing nothing to help him pack up. *Thinks she's so damn smart*.

"You haven't told me where this mine is, you know."

He pulled out his map and spread it on the ground. She bent down beside him. "It's somewhere in this area," he said, pointing to a spot on the map.

She glanced over at him, surprised. "That's awfully vague, isn't it? I thought you knew where this place was supposed to be."

"Well, I do...sort of. According to the research I've done, it has to be right here."

"Uh-huh. Give or take a few miles, you mean?"

"All right, Miss Know-It-All, you tell me. You're the expert on this area, you show me where it is."

She smiled and stood up, dusting her hands together. "I intend to...Fisher. As quickly as possible. Because I am now convinced that that is the only way I'm going to get rid of you."

He sneered at her back. "You're too kind, Miss Holdenfield. And I suppose it would be too much to ask if I could have a cup of your coffee before we start out."

"Help yourself," she called back as she walked off. "I still have to gather up my camera equipment."

"What for?" he called after her.

She turned around and placed her hands on her waist. "Because part of the deal is that if I lead you to your mine, you have to let me get some work done on the way. Agreed?"

"How long is that going to take?"

"Are you in some kind of a race, Fisher?"

"Yeah, something like that."

"Then you may lose it." She smiled and turned away, heading up the slope to her trailer.

Greg threw his jacket down onto the pack that was lying on the ground and then kicked a patch of dirt toward the fire pit. What a disagreeable human being that woman was. He wasn't sure now if he could stand being around her for the few days it would take to find the mine. Maybe he would have been better off to try it on his own. At this point anything looked more enticing than spending several days and nights with that man-hating hermit.

He slowly picked up his pack and held it in his hand as he walked across the meadow to her trailer. He could hear her inside rattling around, so he went over to the stove, dropped his pack on the ground and found an empty cup on the table.

Anne stepped out of the trailer with her pack on and her bag of camera equipment draped over one shoulder. A heavy jacket was tied around her waist. Greg turned and took note of her appearance for the first time today. Her hair was clipped back behind her ears, her face free of makeup and her body covered in form-fitting denims and flannel. Again, despite the soft feminine features, an image of a sturdy pioneer woman came to mind, walking behind a Conestoga wagon, blazing a trail westward across the Continental Divide.

He thought of all the gullible, eager young things he could have been with if he hadn't made this stupid bet. Instead, because he needed the money, he was going to have to trailblaze with Ms. Daniel Boone through the boonies.

She handed him some packets of food and utensils. "Here. You can carry these. Are you ready?" she asked, and he noticed for the first time that her voice didn't quite fit her tough image. It was too quiet and soft, not aggressive enough for one so dominant and strong.

He nodded and set down the cup of coffee. "Ready."

"Okay. Let me see your map again."

Greg pulled it out of the pack's side pocket and spread it out on the table.

"Now," she said, "if you're sure this mine is where you say it is, we've got to go up this way, heading west toward North Baldy. Then we'll go up through Storm Pass and hopefully find your mine. And then," she mumbled to herself, "we can part company."

"How long do you think it will take?"

"That depends."

"On what?"

"On what my sheep are doing. A ram I've been following has been heading that way. It depends on what he does."

Greg rolled his eyes. How long it was going to take depended on what some stupid sheep did! He chuckled lightly. "Listen, Miss Holdenfield..." He laughed again. "I'm sure these sheep are really important to you and all that, but...well, I need to find this mine and be back to Princeton in nine days."

Anne lifted her face to him. He was taller than she by about eight inches, but she wasn't about to be intimidated by this overgrown prep school alumnus standing there in his Izod coordinates. "First of all, Fisher, my work is important to a lot of people, not just me. It takes priority over everything else I do. Now, if that is going to be a problem for you, you can always go back down this mountain and find another guide. If you stay with me and do everything I say, we will try to make it so that you can be home in nine days. If it were up to me, I would like to see you go home today. The last thing I need is some pampered, spoiled Ivy Leaguer tagging along behind me. We will go as fast as we can, but I am going to work along the way. If you are not in agreement with this, you know what you can do about it.''

Greg scowled down at her, his face only inches from hers. "There are words for man haters like you.''

She held her ground. ''All lewd, I am sure.''

He didn't answer for a few seconds, nor did he move away from her. ''If the shoe fits,'' he finally said in a low voice.

Anne grimaced and moved away first. Why did remarks like that always hit so hard? She didn't care what he thought about her. She didn't care what anyone thought. She had spent too many years caring and she was through with all of that. Life on her own terms was the way she wanted it now. No need for a man to direct her every move. And this professor from Princeton was the last person she would let get in her way. Men like him were so sure they knew what women wanted. They were so patronizing and narrow-minded. So who cared what he thought about her; she didn't think much of him, either! That was a lie, but she had been telling herself so many the last few years that one more just added another brick to the wall.

With as little discussion as possible, Anne took the lead and headed up through the thicket of trees to the west. It was a chilly morning and the sun still had a long way to go before it would burn off the early-morning frost and bring much-needed warmth. Anne was used to it; her body had become accustomed to the ways of the high country. But Greg was another story altogether, he was absolutely miserable. His joints ached from the cold, his bones creaked and his fingers and toes kept falling asleep.

After thirty minutes he dropped his pack on the ground and plopped down on a log, his hand pressing against his pain-gripped chest.

When Anne realized he was no longer walking behind her, she stopped. She came back to where he was sitting. "What's the matter?"

He shook his head and tried to gasp for breath. "It's my…how in hell are you supposed to breathe up here? I need a cigarette but I can't seem to catch my breath."

She sniffed disdainfully and sat down beside him. "You'll get used to it." She studied him for a long moment. "You're not in very good shape, are you?"

"I'm in great shape," he gasped.

She laughed. "I can tell." Pulling her canteen out, she offered him a drink, which he gratefully accepted. "Don't you exercise?"

"Exercise?" he asked, as if he had never heard the word before.

"You know, jogging, tennis, swimming, anything."

He shook his head. If he told her what kind of exercise he pursued the most, her puritanical dander would no doubt rise an inch or two. He was starting to feel a little better now. He still couldn't feel his toes inside his boots, but he could at least breathe. He reached into his shirt pocket and pulled out a pack of cigarettes, turned it upside down and dropped several to the moist ground.

"It's no wonder you can't breathe," Anne muttered, watching with distaste as he brushed off one of the cigarettes and lit the end of it with a match. "And what are you going to do with that match?"

He had figured on dropping it to the ground, but at her implied warning he extinguished it and begrudgingly dropped it into his pocket with the pack of cigarettes.

"What do you do for recreation if you don't exercise?" she asked, still unable to believe that anyone could be in that bad shape.

He laughed at the question and then decided it was high time he set this woman straight about a few things. "First of all, I don't exercise. Okay? For recreation, I gamble." He smiled triumphantly at her surprised expression. "And I drink...a lot. And I pick up women in bars." He held up his cigarette. "And I smoke too much. And I have a good time. Now, are you satisfied?" There. He had given it to her straight. That should really get her goat. He couldn't wait to hear what the prude had to say about all of that.

It was with acute disappointment that he watched her stand up without saying a word and move away from him. He stubbed out his cigarette on a rock and, making sure she didn't see him, flipped it into the pine needles at his feet, then hitched up his pack and tried to catch up with her. He fell into step beside her and they walked in silence for a long while, stopping every now and then to let him catch his breath or smoke another cigarette or eat another Milky Way.

Their path began to climb again through the thick stand of trees. Pine and fir and spruce grew tall and spiky, littering the ground with their needles and cones and twigs. Rabbits darted in and out between the trees and a pair of stellar jays squabbled overhead. Kinnikinnick grew in matted clusters in the shade, their round leathery leaves the perfect food for deer, which had left their unique tracks for Anne and Greg to follow.

To Greg, the forest seemed to go on for ever and ever, but finally they reached the edge of it, only to be faced with a bare rock slide that they would have to cross. But the sun was high at this point and the boulders were at least dry to step on.

"We have to reach that ridge up there," she pointed. "Then we'll head down on the other side of this mountain."

"You mean after all this climbing, we have to go down again and then back up?"

"Yes," she said, a smirk creeping across her face. "Wasn't that inconsiderate of nature not to put a level four-lane highway through here so you could simply drive up to your mine?" She didn't hear his muttered reply as she started across the rocks. She wasn't sure why she felt the urge to goad him so much. Of course, he was disrupting her solitude. And he wasn't the least bit interested in her work. And he was out of shape and complained constantly. But even more than that was the fact that he was one of those men who thought they were God's gift to women. Men like him thought that all it took was a smile, a touch, a little sexual dominance to win a woman over. He knew he was good-looking, extraordinarily so, she had to admit. And he thought that was all that mattered. Really, that was why she disliked him so. He was the type of man she wanted to keep away from. She had not been very successful at being a woman, so she had buried that part of her and instead concentrated on being a cool, impartial, impersonal scientist. That way she could not get hurt.

She would not let Greg Fisher uncover what she had so carefully worked to hide.

She had reached the other side of the rock slide and turned around to wait for him. He was making his way across with relative ease, but she knew when he reached her side he would have a million complaints. Unconsciously she smiled at the thought.

And sure enough, when he made it across, he started complaining about everything he could think of. She tried to turn a deaf ear on all his complaints as they continued climbing up toward the ridge. If it wasn't the rocks he complained about, it would be the wet grass, or the cold, or the uncomfortable pack, or the fact that he needed a cigarette, or something. She really didn't care. She wanted to get to the top of the ridge so she could look for Solomon. She hoped he would be down below on the other side and, if so, the gray stone outcropping there would be a perfect place from which to view him.

Greg watched from below as Anne climbed up the steep mountain slope without hesitating, traversing the boulders and uneven terrain like a mountain goat. "That damned woman!" he muttered to himself. There was something so infuriating about her. It was her attitude, to be sure. The way she tilted that arrogant chin up and out at him. The fact that her jeans were tight across the slender curve of her hips and thighs, and she acted as if she didn't know or care that she had a great derriere. And it was also the fact that she wanted him out of her way so she could be alone again. And that it was no trouble at all for her to cross these mountains, while he had to struggle for every breath and every step.

He had never come across anyone like her before. What kind of a woman was she, anyway? Hadn't she ever heard that women were supposed to be soft and cuddly and meek and quiet and all that? Didn't she know that that was what men wanted? Oh, hell, maybe she didn't care. A militant broad like her probably went out of her way to antagonize and provoke men.

He stopped and caught his breath, then trudged up the hill after her. She really was an irksome woman.

He reached the top of the ridge and suddenly felt so dizzyingly proud of himself for making it that he wanted to yodel. But before he could make a sound, Anne hissed at him from behind a large rock.

"Pssst! Shhh!" She signaled him to come toward her. "Stay down low," she whispered furiously and he crouched down against the rocks and scooted over to the lip of the cliff where she was sitting. A few rounded scrubby pine grew out of the tumbles of mossy rocks and hid their presence from the valley below.

"What is it?" he whispered back when he saw her pull out a telescope from her camera bag.

"Solomon. I think he's down there. You've got to stay quiet while I take a look."

"Who the hell is Solomon?"

"My ram."

"Your ram? What is he, some sort of pet?"

She cast a disparaging look at him. "He's a wild bighorn."

"So why does he have a name?"

"I name all the animals I observe. I named all the ewes last year. It makes it easier to keep track of them in my journal."

He shrugged disinterestedly, removed his pack and shook out a cigarette. She slapped the pack of matches from his hand and whispered firmly, "I said be quiet!"

He stared at her for one hostile moment, then put his cigarette carefully back in the pack and leaned back against a rock, his hands cradling his head. He closed his eyes and let the late morning drift around him. The sun was warm on his face and the alpine breeze was cool and fresh. It felt good to lie still, to stop moving for a little while. Maybe he would never move again.

Presently, he opened his eyes to see what Anne was doing. She was in the same position, sitting with her knees bent, faded jeans hugging her hips, the telescope held against her eye with slim fingers, her lithe body and cool expression both motionless.

"You see the old boy?" Greg asked, as his eyes roamed leisurely over her body, cataloguing all the female equipment she tried so hard to keep hidden.

Anne lowered the scope and grabbed her journal and a pencil, hastily writing her observations on the paper. She didn't answer him. In fact, she hadn't even heard him speak. She was so intent on the ram and on pinpointing the location for her journal that she was aware of nothing else. If she had known what he was thinking as he watched her so intently, she would have been highly unnerved. But she didn't know, and so he lay there with his hands clasped behind his head watching her every move, filling his head with all sorts of delightful and erotic imaginings.

After a while he became bored with nothing but mental activity. "Isn't it time to be moving on?" he said, yawning. His body was so tired, he could have stayed here forever, but at this rate he would never find the mine in time.

"Shhh," she answered, waving her hand back at him. "In a minute."

He scooted closer until he was right next to her. "What could possibly be so interesting about one sheep?" he whispered.

"It's very unusual for a ram to break away from his herd and venture off on his own. Usually, four or five males will band together and loaf all summer high in the mountains."

"The bachelor's life," Greg said, a smile on his face. "Sounds pretty good to me."

"That's the point," she said. "His behavior now is more appropriate for the mating season than for the summer."

"I almost hate to ask," he mumbled dryly, "but what is he doing that makes you think that?"

She kept the telescope at her eye as she spoke. "It's a whole display of nervous energy. See the way he keeps stamping his front hoof? And hear that hissing sound? That's a kind of warning they utter when they're pursuing a female. And the other day I watched him battering his horns against a tree and boulder. This causes a secretion from their glands to be sprayed about. It's a way to mark territory. He's definitely out of season."

Greg sniffed. "Sounds to me like he's out of his gourd."

"I don't think so," Anne whispered. "I think he's just searching for something outside the herd of females he was with all winter."

"Like what?"

She shook her head. "I don't know. But that is what I'm going to find out."

Greg sighed. "What if he doesn't go the same direction we're going?"

Anne lowered the scope and raised her chin. "Then we'll detour and follow him."

"But the mine..."

She smiled that superior smile he was beginning to hate. "Let's just hope that the ram decides to go the same way we're going. Oh, look, over there!" She pointed to a spot about twenty feet away.

Greg looked. Some furry brown thing was crawling up a rock to sunbathe. "Ugh. What is that fat, hairy creature?"

"A marmot."

"Wonderful," he mumbled, forgetting his last attempt and pulling another cigarette from his pocket.

Anne's hand came down over his and grabbed the cigarette. "No!" she whispered furiously.

"No what?" he whispered back.

"You'll scare away the marmot if you smoke."

"Tough luck," he said, a little too loudly, and the marmot slunk off under a large boulder to hide.

Anne glared at him. "Now see what you've done. You and your childish nicotine fits."

"Look, lady, my nicotine fits are my business. And if I want to smoke, I damn sure will."

"Not around my animals and not as long as I'm in charge."

Greg moved his face within inches of hers. He could smell a light fragrance of lilac about her, a pleasant, sweet scent that got in the way of his anger. "Well, you are no longer in charge," he uttered between clenched teeth. "I am. I've just mutinied and now I'm in charge."

She lifted her chin, hoping to combat the almost overwhelming power his nearness had over her. "Oh, and suppose I decide to leave and go back to camp? Suppose I tell you that you can find your own way to that mine?"

"You won't."

"I just might. In fact, if you don't stop smoking so much, I definitely will."

"You wouldn't."

Her brown eyes locked with his intense blue ones for a long moment and then her gaze slid to his mouth, held tight in a hard line of contempt. She had to do this for herself as much as or more than for him, so she smiled a slow smile of victory. "Now tell me who is in charge?"

Greg glared into her big brown eyes so close, and he couldn't decide whether to pull her body against his or knock her off the cliff. "Lady," he hissed, "it's no wonder you live up here alone. You are a menace to society."

Chapter Six

They camped that night in a dense grove of spruce. Soft needles and matted vegetation covered the ground beneath the trees, making a perfect spot for a bed. The rest of the afternoon had not gone well at all. From the moment of Greg's foiled mutiny, the climate between the two of them had turned downright chilly. He continued to smoke, but Anne made sure he didn't do it if she was photographing any nearby animals. Now he understood tyranny in its worst form—in the hands of a woman. If there were any way for him to find the mine on his own, he would gladly have relinquished her of her duty.

Anne, on the other hand, was continually disdainful over how out of shape Greg was, over how much he complained and over how much she thought about him. If she could just forget he was tagging along, everything would be fine. But she kept hearing the loud clomp-clomp of his heavy boots behind her. He kept snapping twigs and dry leaves, startling the birds in the trees. She could hear him huffing and puffing. If the man didn't smoke like a chimney, he might have less trouble breathing. Oh, why did he have to come along and screw up her nice, quiet little world? Why doesn't he go back to his singles bars and one-night stands? And why didn't she stop thinking about him?

By nightfall they had very little to say to each other besides a few monosyllabic mutterings. But Greg was by nature a talker, and this overly strained silence eventually got on his nerves.

"Look," he said after dinner, when they were sitting around the fire for warmth and he was drinking from his flask of bourbon. "Can't we find some sort of meeting ground? Call a truce of something?"

Anne sighed heavily. "If you weren't such an annoying man, then—"

"Look, lady," Greg spat. "You ain't so hot yourself."

"You make too much noise," she said, ignoring the interruption. "You talk too much. You complain about everything. You're a slow hiker. You smoke too much. You have an irritating habit of making everything a joke. You have no respect for the environment. You scare away the animals. You're constantly eating candy bars. Why aren't you fat?"

Greg slapped his rock-hard stomach. "High metabolism, I guess."

"See, there you go again, making a joke. Nothing is serious to you, is it?"

"The fact that I am going to win this bet makes my ten grand pretty damn serious. Otherwise, I wouldn't be up in this godforsaken wilderness with an abominable tyrant who thinks she's Davy Crockett, Daniel Boone and Zebulon Pike all rolled into one. Now that's pretty damn serious if you ask me. And yes, I make jokes. But that's better than being an old sour-puss like you. I don't think you've cracked a smile in the three days I've been up here. Your face would probably break if you did. And you think you're so all-fired superior to everyone, don't you? You go tripping across these rocks and hills like you think you're some sort of fawn. Bambi, no doubt. And you act like nothing could ever frighten you or make you slow down." He leaned closer. "You're not afraid of a damn thing, are you?" His voice grew angrier. "Are you?"

Anne sat very still on the log and stared at the fire. An old sourpuss? All-fired superior? Abominable tyrant? Is that the impression she gave? It was so dif-ferent from the view of herself she thought she pre-sented to the world. She would have labeled herself resolute and firm, yes. Perhaps independent and in-telligent, a natural-born leader. But never a sourpuss or a tyrant.

And afraid? Hah, if he only knew. First it was Frank and his constant pressure and assertions that sexuality had no place in a woman of academic sub-stance. Oh, he had given her the satisfaction of being treated as his equal in public, but that was certainly the only satisfaction he had given her. Before the rest of the world, he was the perfect husband; at home, he was a tyrant who expected everything from her ex-cept what she so desperately wanted to give him. And then there was Mamdouh, who had spun her in the opposite direction, caring nothing for her as a person and wanting only her body. When she searched for an equal balance, she always ended up the loser.

Afraid of nothing? Hardly. The thought of being a woman with feelings and a normal sexuality scared the hell out of her. Being a woman meant getting hurt.

She lifted her eyes slowly to Greg. He was sitting a couple of feet away on another log and the firelight gave a warm, yellow glow to his face and eyes and hair. Fighting ferociously against her attempts to keep it hidden away, the woman in her begged to rise to the surface with this man. But the feeling lasted only a second before it froze solid inside her. She swallowed and spoke very softly and slowly. "You are wrong there, Fisher. I'm afraid of more things than you can possibly imagine."

He had been watching her closely and had caught the diverse play of emotions across her face. It was a combination of things—confusion, hurt, anger, self-righteousness. . .fear. And, too, he was probably wrong about this, but he thought he had caught a glimpse of something else in her expression. A kind of seeking out—almost sexual, he would have to say. But no, surely not. Not in Anne Holdenfield's face; he had to be wrong about that.

"I'm afraid of more things than you can possibly imagine." What did she mean by that? There was a vulnerability about her right now that he had not seen before. A weakness she normally kept well hidden.

There were lots of things he wanted to ask her, but he couldn't get rid of this smoldering and, he knew, irrational anger he had for her. It had to do with the way her pretty, well-scrubbed face and slender body

had taunted him all day, the way her strong personality and independence got in the way of his. And it
had to do with the way she looked right now across
the firelight—all soft and vulnerable and very, very
touchable.

"Why aren't you married?" he half grumbled, ir-
ritated with his own mixed-up feelings about her.

She shook her head. "It didn't work out."

"I can't imagine why," he mumbled.

"What did you say?"

"Nothing. Why are you up here, living the way you
do? I mean, you seem like a woman who—if you
don't mind my saying so—thrives on confrontation.
I would think you'd need to be around people more."

Her smile twisted sideways. "And you believe there
isn't much confrontation up here? I would think that
by now you would realize how much there is. Up here
you are faced with the awesomeness of creation every
day. This is an oftentimes hostile environment and
you must become a creature of it. You have to learn
to adapt." She shrugged. "I like that. I like the way
my body responds to the challenge of living up here.
My legs and lungs and arms grow stronger. I learn to
do things I never thought myself capable of doing.

"And I especially like to be alone," she added. "As
Thoreau said, 'I would rather sit on a pumpkin, and
have it all to myself, than to be crowded on a velvet
cushion.'"

"A pumpkin, huh?" he said with a chuckle.

She nodded and smiled. "I like the quiet; it gives
me time to think about...about life and where I fit in
the scheme of things. Most of all I love the animals.

If I could survive the winters up here, I would stay just to study the animals and how they adapt to the constantly changing environment.''

Greg listened, marveling at that kind of dedication and interest in one thing. He had never known that. Oh, he enjoyed teaching and he particularly liked to study history, but he had never felt the kind of satisfaction and sense of purpose that Anne Holdenfield claimed to feel. He had to admit that in a way he was a bit jealous of her.

"How long have you been studying the bighorn sheep?"

"Three years. Last year I watched the females." She laughed softly at some private thought.

"What's so funny?" he wanted to know.

"Oh, I was just thinking about the herd last summer. There were some real characters in that bunch."

"All with names, I suppose."

"Oh, sure," she said. "For example, there was Mrs. Peabody. She was the wise old grandmother who led them all to the best alpine pastures each day and at night, by moonlight, she would cautiously lead them down to water. She was a tough old cookie and she didn't stand for any guff in her herd."

Greg watched her stretch her legs out in front of her and run her hands along the tops of her thighs. "I would think, especially since you name the sheep, you become attached to them and it would be hard to watch them get hurt."

"It is. Disease and parasites take a very heavy toll in the bighorn population. In the old sheep, when their teeth wear down to the gums, they slowly starve. And there is nothing we humans can do about that."

"I don't know too much about bighorn sheep other than what I see on the television truck commercials." He laughed at Anne's expression. "You know, where they bang their horns together."

"I must have missed that one," she murmured with a chuckle. "But I have seen the real thing. When two males are interested in the same female, a violent duel of horns takes place. It's a magnificent sight."

"What will you do after the summer is over?" Greg asked.

"Well, I'll finish my thesis and then I'll probably work with the forest service in wildlife habitat research."

"You don't want to teach?"

She smiled at the thought. "No, I don't think I could handle that. I don't have the patience with people that I do with animals."

How true he knew that to be, but he didn't say so. Instead, he was watching how the light from the fire played with the color of her hair. Her skin glowed warm and golden, and every time she looked at him her brown eyes burned holes right through him, igniting the blood in his veins to fever pitch.

"Don't you ever get lonely?" he asked.

She glanced up. "For other people?"

His eyes narrowed on her face, more open and receptive tonight than she had been since he'd met her. Then his gaze slid in a long, easy trail down her body. He lifted them once again to her face. "For a man."

She was silent for a long time, afraid to answer, afraid to even think about it. She was past all that. She had found her niche in life and she was content with it. Passion was the key that unlocked the door to hurt. She wanted no part of it.

And yet this man sitting only a few feet away— handsome, young, virile, full of unlimited sexual steam and bold self-confidence, with blue eyes that sparkled with passion and the promise of fun—was asking her a question like that. How on earth was she supposed to answer? She wasn't about to expound on her personal survivalist philosophy of life, or detail all of her past failures with men. What was she to say? She didn't want him to think she was attracted to him, so she had to step carefully there. Why, the very idea of it was absurd! He was the antithesis of what she had always been drawn to. He was just out for another sexual romp anyway. She wasn't too blind to see that. Women were obviously nothing more than chattels to him, trappings of pleasure. No, she had to steer clear of this man's abundant sexual charm. As tempting as it and he might be, she wasn't about to fall into his trap.

"You haven't answered my question," he said, watching her closely.

She stood up and dusted the seat of her pants. "And I have no intention of answering it, Fisher."

"Don't you think you should call me Greg?"

"Why?"

He shrugged. "It's my name. Of course, if you'd rather call me Ralph or Fred or Carbunkle or something, that's okay. Just anything but Fisher. The way you say it makes me feel like some sort of mad, hunchbacked scientist lumbering along behind you.''

Anne smiled down at him and couldn't stop the laugh that bubbled up. There was something about him that was so... Oh, damn, she wished he hadn't come up here and upset her equilibrium this way. ''Okay, Carbunkle,'' she said, chuckling. ''Now you'd better hit the sack. You've got a big day ahead of you tomorrow.''

He stood up and reached for his backpack, but he didn't take his eyes off her. ''You know,'' he said, ''you should smile more often. You're very pretty when you smile.''

Anne turned away and rummaged through her pack, keeping her back to him the whole time. Why did she have to smile, dammit? She didn't want to give him any more ammunition than he already had. She grabbed a towel, a bar of soap and some fresh clothes and stood up.

''Where are you going?''

She looked back over her shoulder. ''To take a bath.''

''Tonight?''

''Yes.''

''In the dark?''

''Yes, Fisher. I like it better at night.'' She couldn't stop the playful grin. ''No Peeping Toms that way.''

''What about all those animals out there lurking in the bushes?'' he said. ''Peering at you with their red, beady eyes.''

She stared at him in amazement. ''What kinds of books do you read!''

"Won't it be cold in the water?" he asked, still trying to fathom this whole procedure of hers.

"Probably. Now may I go?"

He grinned mischievously. "Want some help?"

"Thanks, but I've been taking my own baths since I was five. Of course, if you'd like to follow my lead and take one when I'm through..."

"Are you kidding! No way am I going out there in the dark and sitting in an icy stream. I'll wait until morning, thank you."

She flipped the towel over her shoulder and started toward the creek. "Suit yourself."

He watched her as she waded through the high grass that surrounded the stream. The willow bushes gave her some privacy, but with the moon full above them and the sky brilliant with starlight, he was still able to see her silhouette as she dropped her shirt and jeans and lifted the thin camisole over her head. The bank sloped toward the stream and once she stepped down into the water, he could no longer see her from the camp.

With a heavy exhalation of breath, he spread out his bedroll. Last night he had been in a tent. Tonight he would be out in the open, available to any wild animal that might come along for a midnight snack. The thought made him uneasy at best.

He picked up the corner of his sleeping bag and dragged it over next to hers.

Following her advice of that morning, he removed his clothes and let the down material hold his body heat in the bag. He lay down and closed his eyes, but sleep would not come. He kept picturing her through the swaying willows under the moonlight, lifting that thin piece of nylon over her head. She was such a strange creature. On the outside she was denim and flannel. So durable, so tough, so hard in many ways. And yet, beneath it all was a pink camisole, a softness, a femininity that was all but hidden from the rest of the world. And that smile! What a surprise that had been. He had just about decided that she was incapable of it. He had told her she was pretty when she smiled, but in truth she was more than that. She had a kind of subtle beauty about her that was very much like the natural phenomena that surrounded her. It was another facet of Anne Holdenfield that she tried to hide from the seeing world. But tonight he had caught a glimpse of it. And for some reason he couldn't fathom, he was not going to let her hide it again.

With his hands behind his head, he searched the night sky for familiar constellations. There was Perseus straight overhead and Cassiopeia in the east. The Big Dipper and the North Star were hidden behind the towering mountains, and he could just see a tiny bit of Andromeda in the west.

He glanced toward the stream where Anne was now bathing. Andromeda, chained and at the mercy of some unseen monster. He smiled to himself. It would be easy to see her as that and him as her Perseus, rescuing her from a fate worse than death. He sniffed derisively at the notion. No, she didn't seem to find life without a man all that horrible. He thought he knew women. He thought he had been around. But maybe there were some who eluded his formula.

Nah, what's the matter with you, Fisher? If anyone knows women, it's you, old boy. You have been around and you have definitely got them pegged.

With a smile and that final reassuring thought, Greg Fisher dropped off to sleep.

ANNE EASED DOWN into the icy water. It pricked and stung her skin as it swirled around her, tumbling and sliding over the slick granite rocks, and it was several minutes before she grew numb to the chilling ache. She had pulled the band from her ponytail and now leaned her head way back to wet her hair. It floated on top of the stream and her scalp tingled from the refreshing cold.

Clusters of stars were thick overhead and she lay back, watching them as the eddies of crystal-clear water swirled like the maddening caress of a man's fingers around and over her body. His fingers and hands—she wondered what they would feel like against her skin, touching her and making her come alive.

She splashed water on her face and wondered what he thought about her. He had said she was pretty when she smiled, but did he really think so?

Her thoughts began to tumble and slide with the spring water as she washed her hair and body, reveling in the caress of the icy stream and the fantasy of Greg Fisher's hands running over her. Maybe he thought she needed makeup. Maybe she was too plain....

Dammit, Anne! What are you thinking! She quickly rinsed off and stood up, moving to the bank for her towel. She was insane, she really was. How could she let some total stranger affect her this way? She didn't want to have anything to do with him, she insisted as she slipped into her clothes and gathered up her things. She didn't even like the man.

She stopped and sighed, lifting her head to stare up at the all-seeing night sky. Well, she finally admitted to the stars and to herself, okay, so maybe she did like him—she lowered her head and started walking toward the camp—but only just a little. And that was never going to change. She would make sure of it.

Chapter Seven

Once again a sharp jab to the rib cage was his introduction to the morning.

"Damnation, woman! Are you going to do that every morning? It's no wonder you're no longer married," he grumbled, sitting up in the bedroll and then immediately sliding back under the warm down cover.

"Come on, Nanook of the North," Anne said with a laugh, tossing his clothes on top of him. "It's time to get moving."

"I'm sleeping in this morning," he said beneath the cover.

"Suit yourself, but I'm taking off in fifteen minutes...with or without you."

He flipped back the cover to his waist and glared at her. "You're such fun to be with."

She successfully ignored his gibe but she could not ignore his lean bare torso as she went about heating some freeze-dried eggs for his breakfast. He had that warm, sleep-tousled look, and she wondered what it would feel like to run her hands along that warm, hard chest.

He pulled his jeans under the cover and slipped them on, standing up to fasten them. She tried to keep her eyes on the skillet and off his hands as they slid the zipper up to the snap. She forced herself to look at his face and, to her acute embarrassment, realized that he had been watching her—and he clearly knew that she had been watching him.

His smile was warm and intimate, but he relieved her of her embarrassment by kneeling down and digging through his pack for fresh clothes and bath supplies. "I'm going to brave that bathtub," he said as he stood up. "Keep my breakfast warm, squaw," he called over his shoulder as he headed for the water.

"Anything you say, Kimo Sabe," she mumbled behind his back, vastly relieved that he was gone and she could regain her composure.

He walked to the spot where he had watched her undress the previous night, pulled his jeans off and sat on the bank, grimacing as he stuck one foot in the icy water. Goose bumps immediately covered his skin, and it took tremendous willpower to force himself to stick his other foot in the stream. After a couple of minutes his feet were completely numb from the cold, and he decided to venture in a little farther.

Anne looked up once from her cooking, but he was hidden behind the willows. When she heard a loud wail, she covered her mouth to stifle the laughter and knew that he had finally made it into the water.

When he came back to the camp her gear was already packed and she had charted their route for the day.

"Be forewarned," he said between chattering teeth as he walked up. "That may be the last one of those I take on this trip."

"Sit down and get warm by the fire," she said, laughter in her voice. "You'll feel better in a minute." She stared at him for too long and knew that she had to do something to get her mind on the right track. Why did he have to stand there with that wet, gleaming bare chest? He was doing that on purpose, she decided angrily. He knew she was attracted to him and he was going to play it for all it was worth. Well, she would just show him that she wasn't affected by his little performance. "You haven't told me much about this mine you're looking for. How did you hear about it?" There, see, she could carry on a normal conversation quite easily. She wasn't affected in the least.

Greg slipped on a shirt, then sat down on the log and tried to warm his frozen skin. His hair was damp and clung to his neck, and he shivered as he rubbed his hands together. If he realized that she had asked the question to get more personal thoughts off her mind, he showed no evidence of it. "We were talking about the mining days in one of my classes a few months back," he said. "We were talking about some of the famous lost mines—the Lost Dutchman, the Hole-in-the-Sky, a few others."

Anne noticed the sheepish look that crossed his face as he buttoned the cuffs of his flannel shirt.

"Anyway," he said shrugging. "I made the mistake of saying that I could find any of these lost mines. That all it would take was some research, and I could find anything."

Her tone became cooler and more detached as she tried to erect a new barrier between them. "And someone took you up on it?"

He ran his fingers through his damp hair. "Yeah, three graduate students who spend more time finding ways to annoy me than studying."

"You got a bet for ten thousand dollars from graduate students?"

"Very rich graduate students."

"Obviously," she mumbled in disapproval. "Here, take this plate. I'm tired of holding it."

Greg took the plate of food and starting eating, but after the first bite made a horrible face. "What is this supposed to be?"

"Eggs."

He looked down at the plate and frowned. "Really?" He dug through them with his fork. "Could have fooled me."

"So why did you take these students up on the bet?" she asked impatiently.

He heard the whiplike snap in her voice and took note of the sudden change in her expression. *There she goes again,* he thought. *She's clamming up on me again.* He took a bite of toast. "I needed the money," he said.

"Why?"

He set his fork down on the tin plate and stared at her. She looked great that morning. All rosy and fresh

and full of energy. Too bad she had to act so damned
snooty all of a sudden. "You sure do ask a lot of
questions."

She shrugged. "I'm inquisitive by nature."

"I've got some debts to pay off," he replied
offhandedly.

"Buy why would you make a bet to do something
you don't know how to do? For heaven's sake, Fisher,
you don't even know how to read a compass. I
watched you yesterday and you are out of your league. Weren't you ever a Boy Scout?"

He chewed on the rubbery eggs and swallowed
them in a lump before answering. "I was kicked out."

Anne rolled her eyes and sighed. "What for?"

He took a bite of the beef jerky that lay alongside
the eggs. "Sneaking into the Girl Scouts' tent on a
camp-out."

She pursed her lips and shook her head. "That fig-
ures." Sitting on the log beside him, she silently
watched him eat his food. "Finished?"

"Yeah, but what's the rush?"

She stood up and reached for his empty plate. "I
want to see what Solomon is doing today," she said
as she walked toward the creek to wash the plates.

"How long is that going to take?" he called after
her, but she didn't answer. "What's so great about
this crazy sheep anyway? Sounds to me like he just
needs a good..."

"A good what?" she asked, coming back to the
camp and stowing the plate in her pack. She glared up
at him. "What crude expression were you going to use
there?"

He lifted the pack to his shoulders. "What I meant was that I think he needs a girlfriend. That's probably his problem."

"Oh, I see. You've been studying the Rocky Mountain bighorn for so long that you've got it all figured out."

"Well, what else could it be?" he answered defensively. "It's either that or he's nuts. And why should you waste your time or mine chasing after some horny sheep?"

Anne had slipped on her pack and was now standing with her hands on her waist as she stared at him. She was not going to feel anything but irritation for this man. No matter how good he looked or how evocative his smile might be, she was not. "Fisher, have I told you how annoying you are?"

"A few times."

"Good. Then I won't bother to say it again. Let's go."

IT WAS A COLD, CRYSTAL MORNING and the trees and grass sparkled with dew. The forest buzzed with the busy activities of squirrels and chipmunks and woodpeckers, while the meadow sang with the chorus of finches and robins and jays.

They climbed higher and higher through the sloping pastures, up over jagged ridges and across the tumbles of rock slides. And with each step, Greg had to struggle harder for every breath. Without conscious effort and out of sheer necessity, he had cut down on his smoking; he simply didn't have the oxygen for it.

Their pants legs were soaked to the knees from the wet, marshy meadows and willow fields. When he had the breath to ask, Anne pointed out the varieties of grasses and flowers, the bright yellow skunk cabbage, lily of the valley, white-blossoming bur reed. Otherwise she said nothing much at all. She was intent on finding the ram and didn't want to be bothered with his small talk.

She was more irritable than normal that morning and she knew why. She blamed it on the fact that he kept snapping so many twigs as he walked, but she knew that had nothing to do with it. What really bothered her was the fact that she was beginning to like him. Really like him. But how could that be? How could she possibly feel any attraction or friendship for this thirty-six-year old adolescent? She was just going to have to try harder to keep her mind on her work, where it belonged. Then and only then would she be safe.

Greg, walking along minding his own business and looking down at his feet, didn't realize that Anne had stopped, when he ran smack into the back of her. Cold disdain in her expression was his reward for that little faux pas.

"What did you stop for?" he complained.

"Shhh, look."

He followed the line of her finger to the tuft of grass and pine needles beneath a tree. Something moved, but just barely. "What is it?" he whispered.

"Snowshoe hare. A young one." Very slowly, she pulled her camera from its case and lifted it to her eye, working on the focus.

"I thought they were white," he said softly.

She adjusted the focus. "Only in the winter. The winter molt to white doesn't begin until about mid-September." She clicked the shutter, then refocused and took another shot. A bird fluttering in the top of the tree frightened the hare and it dove for cover. Anne lowered her camera and stowed it back in its case. "This is the first one I've seen up here this summer. They're largely nocturnal animals and usually stay hidden in snug little hideouts during the day."

"You say that rabbit was a baby?"

She glanced over at him with that superior look he had come to know so well. "Not rabbit, Fisher. Hare. There's a difference. And yes, it was probably about seven or eight weeks old."

He yawned as a direct retaliation against her didactic tone of voice with him. "Well, let's get going," he said. "We're never going to find the mine at this rate."

"So what's the deal with this mine anyway?" she grumbled as they started walking again. "You haven't told me anything about it."

He glanced over at her, surprised. "I didn't think you were interested."

She looked up and her eyes caught his; a white-hot jolt of electricity shot through her. She fought it down. "I'm not. Just being polite, that's all."

He looked away. "Well, don't bother."

She sighed deeply. "Okay, Fisher, I'm curious. Are you happy now?"

He smiled to himself as his mind formed the image of him making little chinks in the wall she had erected between them. "What do you want to know?"

"Where did the name come from?" she asked, thinking he must need some specific question to get started. She wished now she had never even brought it up.

"It was given to the mine by the townspeople of Castleton and Baldwin. And none of them ever even saw it."

"Who mined it?"

"Well, it seemed there was this grizzled prospector by the name of Pervis 'Stoneface' Johnson—back then they often nicknamed people according to their disposition...." He narrowed his eyes on her. "Not a bad idea," he speculated aloud. "I can think of one or two people that appellation might fit."

Anne turned her head toward him and searched for a teasing glint in his eyes. She saw none. Well, good, she thought defensively. If it took the hard line to keep him at bay, then fine.

"Anyway," Greg continued. "Old Pervis came to Colorado around 1880, took himself a Ute squaw and headed up into the high country in search of gold."

"Took himself a Ute squaw," she scoffed. "No wonder you like this story. You probably love all the old Tarzan movies, too, don't you?"

Greg puffed out his chest. "Me Tarzan, you Jane."

She shook her head and tried not to smile. *Dream on, Fisher. That would be the day!* The day she fell for that macho, chauvinistic bunk was the day she was going to have herself committed to an asylum.

He studied her for a minute, walking so erect and haughty beside him. What was it about this woman that kept getting under his craw? And why didn't all the old standard lines and moves work on her?

He turned his attention back to the story. "There really wasn't too much in the literature about him. What little background there was on the man showed that he came from 'back East' and some notations claimed he was a doctor who had lost his license." He laughed. "One book supported claims that he was the brother of Alferd Packer come West to finish the meal his brother had started."

"What!" She turned a horrified face toward him. "How disgusting! What's so funny?"

"Oh, I was just thinking about my students. You know how college kids are. They have this rather sick, macabre sense of humor, and they loved the story about how Packer hatcheted and ate seven men in the frozen wilderness."

She gave him a serious look. "You must be a very sick teacher."

Her criticism bounced right off him. "Yep, seems that once young Alferd Packer scooted back from the table, there twern't much left."

"Oh, please," she said, laughing yet trying to make it appear more like a groan, "would you get on with the story?"

He watched her tilt her head back to laugh, her hair cascading down her back across the pack, her voice husky and low. And something happened. It was some natural sexual urge to be sure, but it was also something more. *Fisher,* he warned himself, *things*

*are going well for you at this stage of your life. You've
got all the women you need and want. Don't get
yourself messed up in a situation you don't really
want.*

"Okay," he said, clearing his throat to pull his
mind back on track. "So nobody knew much about
this Pervis Johnson fellow. He left only a trail of
mystery and wild reports in his wake. The first report
that he had discovered a mine was in 1882, when he
walked into a saloon in Castleton and quietly ordered a round of drinks for everyone."

Anne felt her interest growing as she listened. She
was really surprised, too. Greg Fisher had a unique
ability to draw vivid verbal pictures. Any teacher who
could make history come alive was rare indeed. She
had not been able to picture him in that role before
now.

"Well," he continued, "you can imagine how the
curiosity of these townsfolk in the bar was aroused
when they learned that this sober-looking man with
long, flaming-red hair had hit a big one. Gold assay-
ing out at a thousand dollars to the ton, he told them."

"Nice little gold mine there," she murmured.

"I'll say. And by the time old Stoneface finished
with his story, those men were probably drooling in
their drinks over the prospects of cashing in on some
of that ore. But apparently when they asked where the
mine was, Pervis simply replied, 'Up yonder.'"

She narrowed her eyes on him. "Did you make that
up, Fisher?"

He smiled enigmatically. "Well...I'm sure he said
something like that."

Anne rolled her eyes.

"And when they wanted to know how to get to the mine, old Pervis said, 'Dunno. I jest smelt my way up thur. Don't fer certain knowed if ah'll ever git back up thur ur not. 'Tain't takin' nobodies with me, neither.'"

Anne laughed out loud, then covered her mouth when she realized how many animals she must have scared away with the noise. "You missed your calling," she stated in a half-accusatory tone.

"Stand-up comedian on 'The Tonight Show'?" he asked hopefully.

"Actually I was thinking of one of those lounge lizards at a local Holiday Inn."

He grinned at the image. "Great, I have a future after all. Now, tell me you're not intrigued by this legend of the mine."

Anne's chin shot out in defense. "I couldn't care less, really. I was just trying to be polite." She turned away, but his hand on her arm stopped her in midstride. She was spun around and his right hand closed over her other arm.

He was looking down at her seriously, unsmiling. Suddenly, her answer had become very important to him. "Tell me you're intrigued," he said, looking down into her face.

His hands were sliding up and down her arms, slowly and gently. She tried to breathe, but there suddenly didn't seem to be enough oxygen in the air between them. His hand slid up to her shoulder, then his fingers spread around the base of her neck, his thumb pressing her chin upward.

Intrigued? she wondered. *By what? How can I answer that question truthfully? Yes, I'm intrigued. By his story. And by him.* She moistened her lips as she tried to form the words, but before she could utter a sound, his head lowered and his mouth moved over hers like the soft breath of the pine trees. *He doesn't have a serious thought in his head,* she warned herself. *All he cares about is drinking and smoking and gambling and picking up women in bars. He is a far cry from the man of your dreams, Anne.*

His mouth against hers, so persuasive and warm, sent a thrill of longing through her that she was not sure she could contain. Her hands lifted to his chest, her fingers pressed against the soft material of his shirt. No, he was wrong for her. But yes—heaven help her—she was intrigued.

"We'll never get to your mine at this rate," she offered weakly against his mouth.

His hand slid down her arm and curved into her waist. He smiled gently down at her. "Could be worth losing the bet over."

She tried to even out her breathing as she stared at the hollow in his throat. "Don't be so sure. I'm not that wonderful."

His hand slipped around to her hip and he pulled her up closer to him. "Who says?"

She wanted to let herself go. She wanted to fall into the fragrant meadow of this man's arms and let him draw the woman out of her. But emotional survival had been her major goal for too long now. She could not let herself lose everything over one man.

She stepped back, gaining emotional as well as physical distance. "Take my word for it, Fisher," she said softly. "And...I think we'd better continue on our way. I...uh...I want to find Solomon before the morning is over."

He reluctantly loosened his hold on her and let her slip away from him. But he frowned as she started walking at a brisk pace. Why did she constantly erect these barriers? And why was she putting herself down like that? The real question, he knew, was why did he care if she did or didn't? She wasn't the type of woman he was attracted to. It was just because she was here and he was here and there wasn't any better choice around. That was all it was. Surely. Oh, she was pretty, yes—beautiful, even. And she felt good in his arms.

But she was so damn independent. And too strong. And too...well, too much of an equal. He was supposed to be the dominant one. That was the way it had been in all of his relationships before. He was the man, the leader, the guiding force, the aggressor, the conqueror and the reaper of all spoils. With this woman, he was always off balance, always less than the absolute victor. He wasn't at all sure he liked that. That wasn't the way the game was played. What was the matter with her anyway? Didn't anybody ever bother to teach her the rules between men and women?

"Aren't you going to finish the story?" she tentatively asked when they were once again on their way. He was too quiet, and she didn't even want to speculate on what he was thinking about.

"Where was I?" he asked, not showing much interest in the story anymore.

"Pervis Johnson told the townspeople that he wasn't going to take them with him to the mine, or something to that effect." She smiled almost shyly. "It loses something in the translation."

Greg caught the smile and returned it. Maybe she couldn't help herself. Maybe she just needed someone to show her how the game between men and women was played. Someone to teach her the rules. Maybe him.

His chest expanded with the powerful, ego-building thought. If Anne Holdenfield wanted to learn the game, he was the best teacher she could find.

"Well," he said, focusing his thoughts on the story of the mine. "Pervis said he smelt his way and smelling their way to a mine was not something these men had ever thought of before. And I don't suppose they took too kindly to the miner's inhospitable remark of going it alone, either. So, apparently, they decided among themselves that they would follow him up into the mountains, staying far enough back so he wouldn't know they were there but close enough to keep track of him."

"And did they find it?"

"Now this is where it gets difficult to separate fact from fiction. Over the years the tale was elaborated upon so much, and grew to such mystical proportions, that it's hard to know what actually happened. But a group of men did follow the red-haired prospector up into the mountains. They kept climbing higher and higher, day after day, until they reached timberline. But old Pervis didn't stop there. He just kept on going farther and farther, higher and higher, up the bare, jagged peaks, as fleet and sure-footed as Anne Holdenfield, no doubt.''

She took that as a compliment and smiled. It was the first nice thing he had said to her. Or maybe it was just the first one she heard and accepted.

"They were within sight of him, or so the story goes, and then suddenly something happened.''

He paused dramatically and Anne turned to him expectantly, captivated and most definitely intrigued.

" 'It was like the sky just opened up and swallowed him,' one of the men reportedly said. Pervis 'Stone-face' Johnson, who was only a few hundred yards up above them, just poof. . .disappeared.'' Greg shrugged. "So the half-dozen sullen men who had followed him up there just returned to Castleton, no doubt bewildered and frustrated over their attempts to find what Johnson claimed to be 'the richest mount'n o' gold this side of hiven.'''

Anne turned to him with a grin. "Is that what he claimed?''

Greg clicked his teeth. "Yep, that's what he claimed.''

"And no one ever found the mine later?''

"Well, Pervis apparently returned to the valley many times after that. And many men tried to follow him back up into the mountains. But at that same spot up there, he would simply disappear above them into that hole in the sky. It was, let's see. . .1887, I think, when Johnson was last seen. He had been mining up there and coming down to town every few months for five years. But he either died or moved on, because no one ever saw him again, nor did they ever pinpoint the location of his mine."

Anne looked over at him. "But you insist it's there."

Greg thought about that a minute. "Let me put it this way: If it is there, I intend to find it."

"All by yourself," Anne smirked.

He grinned. "With a little help from my friends."

Friends. He said it. But she knew there was no possibility of that. The strange and exciting impulses inside her body told her that she was beyond that stage. And if she wanted to get through these few days in one piece, she would have to stay very cool and impersonal with him.

Despite all these good intentions, Anne found herself talking more and more to Greg as the morning wore on. She would point out some of the more interesting geological formations and explain the irregularities in the landscape. They passed several active beaver ponds where lodges of six feet or more in height had been built. The backed-up water behind the dams saturated the soil beneath them, making way for such water-loving plants as willows, alders, cottonwoods and aspens. But on this day no beaver were to be seen.

Every so often Anne would stop to photograph something that had caught her eye or jot down notes in her journal. When they stopped by a creek for lunch, she spent several minutes writing in the notebook.

"What do you write about?" he asked after watching her for a while.

She didn't answer for a minute. Her journal was the closest thing to her mind and to her soul. She wasn't at all sure that Greg should know that. "Oh," she answered evasively, "it's a combination of scientific data and...and personal observations."

"About what?"

She searched for some pat, inconsequential answer. "I'm trying to keep track of what it is that characterizes the alpine ecosystem. I'm trying to learn what it takes for plants and animals to survive above timberline."

He was watching her closely. Something had made her clam up again. Was he getting too personal? What was she so afraid of? "And what have you learned?" he asked, unable to hold back. For the first time he could ever remember, he wanted to see beneath the surface of a woman; he wanted to know what made her tick.

She gave some bland and dogmatic scientific answers about rapid loss of heat and water from organisms, about solar radiation and fewer molecules to hold in the heat, but he really wasn't paying much attention. He managed to insert some provocative questions, as if he knew or cared what the hell she was talking about. But his mind wasn't on the topic at hand. Instead, his every nerve ending was honed in on her face, flushed and glowing and beautifully natural. On her body, gently curved and totally female beneath the heavy layers of clothing. He focused on her voice, low and clear and so intense on what she was saying.

He regarded her for a long moment. "You like what you do, don't you?"

"Of course," she said, surprised that he would even ask such a silly question. "Don't you?"

He shrugged. "I don't know. It's...it's just what I do." He turned the subject back to her. "Maybe you'll let me read your journal sometime," he ventured softly, pulling a cigarette from his shirt pocket and sticking it unlit between his lips.

She was unable to pull her eyes away. Even that irritating smoking habit of his had taken on a sensual significance. Everything he did, every move he made, every sound he uttered made her aware that he was totally male in every sense of the word.

She watched mesmerized as he pulled out a book of matches, struck one and lit the end of the cigarette. With his eyes narrowed, he watched her through the veil of smoke, and this time when he dropped the match to the ground, she didn't even notice.

"Do I fit in there somewhere?" he asked, sticking the matchbook back into his pocket.

"In where?" she half croaked.

"In your journal."

She swallowed hard and pulled her eyes away from him, busying her hands with the packing up of their lunch. "I was instructed to keep a daily log of everything that went on in my life up here." Her attempt to sound pragmatic and impersonal was strained at best.

Greg took a deep draw on his cigarette, then stubbed it out on a nearby rock. They didn't taste as good up this high and besides that he didn't have the oxygen to inhale. "You could omit things you don't want to include," he said. "You could pretend that certain things never happened, that certain people didn't come along. No one would ever know."

She contemplated the idea and the man as she looked over at him. "That would be dishonest."

He shrugged. "Only to yourself. And some of us lie to ourselves all the time."

Anne quickly stood up and pulled on her pack. She was not going to discuss this any further. He was getting too personal, too close to the truth, and he was touching too many exposed nerves. She had to put an end to it. Now.

They hiked in relative silence for a couple more hours, stopping every so often to rest. By midafternoon, they were climbing across a hogback ridge near the Continental Divide and Anne began issuing strict orders to stay low and stay quiet. They moved slowly across the dizzying crest, hunkering down low behind jagged boulders or gnarled and twisted trunks of pine that had been battered by the fierce winds. Anne kept her scope within easy reach, scanning every cleft and gully and chink in the landscape for the lone ram.

Finally she spotted him. She sat down on a boulder and Greg squatted on his heels beside her. He could feel the excitement emanating from her body. It lifted from her in a glowing wave, and he couldn't take his eyes off her face. Forgetting herself for a moment, she turned and smiled at him, and he realized he had never seen her look so beautiful, so alive and radiant. In fact, he didn't think he had ever seen any woman look as beautiful as she did right then. The spark he had been hoping to see in her was now burning full and bright.

She pulled her scope from the pack and surveyed the meadow below them, trying to zero in on the movement she had seen a moment before. But she was aware of Greg's eyes on her, burning through her and igniting her nerve endings. He was so close and the afternoon was so warm and enticing. She was excited to spot the ram, but it was nothing compared to the intoxication she felt at having this thoroughly masculine man so near. She wanted to jump out of her skin when he reached around her for the other set of binoculars, his arm grazing her back and waist.

He lifted them to his eyes and scanned the lower plateau. "What is that?" he whispered.

"What?"

"Look right down there through that gulch. In that thick patch of brush."

Anne followed his directions and aimed her scope into the brush. A sharp intake of breath followed as she focused on the movement.

It was another sheep, a ewe with a patch of white on her left flank and slightly backward-curving spike horns, coming out of a dense patch of fir and spruce. "Oh, Greg!" Anne whispered excitedly, laying her hand against his leg. "Look!"

The female sheep moved toward Solomon, and he stood still. He made a hissing sound through his nose and stomped his forefoot. The ewe uttered a doglike barking sound, indicating an uneasiness but not nec-essarily something she considered dangerous.

Greg's blood began to pound as he watched the scene in front of him. His leg was on fire where Anne's hand rested and he dropped his own hand over it, curling his fingers around hers. While all of their senses were tuned to that spot on his leg, their eyes re-mained fixed on the meadow below them.

The ewe backed away and the ram moved toward her, curling his lip back to expose his teeth and sniff-ing the air. She was standing still now and he moved up behind her. His front leg stretched out and gently touched her hind one. He pushed her hip with his nose once and she jumped back, bleating. The ram whis-tled through his nose and stamped his front foot loudly. He pushed against her again, and this time she did not jump away. He continued to gently shove her with his nose and nibbled on her back and flank whenever she stopped.

Greg slowly lifted Anne's hand to his lips and his mouth moved leisurely down the length of each fin-ger. He turned her hand over and his lips followed the fingers back down to the center of her palm.

Anne felt the pounding of her heart and a rush of longing poured through her. But she did not look at him. She could not take her eyes off the slow ritualis-tic dance of mating that was taking place between the two sheep.

And so, with Greg's mouth burning the flesh of her palm, they both watched mesmerized as Solomon slowly and carefully drove his ewe into the dense cover of trees.

Anne's hand was lowered back to his leg, a little higher on his thigh this time. She lowered her scope and stared straight ahead, expelling a ragged breath. Finally, she turned and looked at Greg.

"What did I tell you?" he said smiling, his voice husky and warm in the afternoon air. "Your ram was on the make and he's been out scoping the territory for action."

Anne slowly shook her head as she stared into his sky-blue eyes. "This is the lambing season," she argued. "The males don't even associate with the females in summer. This isn't the mating season."

Her eyes were big and brown and full of wonder, and he knew he had never wanted a woman so much in his life as he wanted this one right now. He wrapped his big hand around the back of her neck and lifted her chin up toward him, his voice low and dominant. "You may know a lot about alpine ecosystems, Anne Holdenfield. But you sure don't know much about the birds and the bees." He cocked his head slightly as he looked down at her mouth, so moist and pliable, and felt her breath quick and warm against his neck. "Didn't you know? It's always the mating season."

She stared up at him, and the power of his voice and the feel of his hands rocked her to her very foundations. She had tried to resist him. She had tried to retain her emotional footing. She had tried so hard. But looking now into the deep blue depths of his eyes, she knew she had lost. She lost all footing and felt her senses slip into his control, and she realized with an almost exquisite pain that this was where she wanted to be. "All this time," she whispered breathlessly, "Solomon's been looking for a mate. Why didn't I know that?"

His head lowered, his mouth only inches from hers, and his eyes raked across her face with an intensity that stopped her heart. "You should have," he said, his voice low and husky and very seductive. "It's a universal quest."

Chapter Eight

It was night. The fire had burned down to a low, warm glow that crackled and popped as the logs smoldered to ash. Anne finished writing in her journal to the light of her flashlight, then closed the notebook and stowed it in her pack, along with the two metal plates, now clean from their dinner. She glanced over at Greg lying on his bedroll, hands folded behind his head as he looked up at the sky. Her eyes lifted to the stars above, then back to him. She took a deep breath and stood up. "Think I'll go for a short walk."

He turned his head and looked over at her but didn't answer. She left the camp and started walking toward the trees, where she could be insulated from the night and the man and the feelings she did not want to face. All the rest of the afternoon and evening she had tried to buffer herself against them. And all afternoon and evening she had failed miserably. When he kissed her that afternoon, she knew she had lost. They both knew it, and yet he had deliberately pulled back, giving her space and time to work out her feelings toward him.

She did not want to be attracted to this man. She did not even want to like him. But she did. He was funny and handsome and talkative and so utterly full of himself. And even when he was dead wrong about something and knew it, he would stubbornly insist that he was right. And he still complained all the time, although she realized now it was mostly just to goad her on. He argued with her constantly for the same reason. He was a challenge, this man was. He was different. Unique. Fresh. But, oh, he had been such a nuisance. How could she forget that? How could she fall for someone like that!

Greg had given her the afternoon and evening to think about it. She was glad of that because it had given her the chance to regain her emotions and come to a decision. She was going to have to hold on, that's all. With any luck just a few more days, and then he would be gone, out of her hair, out of her life, out of her mind.

The farther into the forest she walked, the more she realized that she was fooling herself. She wasn't going to hold on, she had not recaptured her emotions, and she had certainly not come to the decision that would protect her heart. She stopped and leaned against a tree, wanting the forest to swallow her up, wanting it to offer an escape from the inevitability of what she knew she would end up doing. She couldn't resist him. She had tried and lost. And the realization of all that entailed terrified her.

GREG HAD WATCHED Anne walk into the forest and he wondered if he should follow her. He wasn't comfortable enough with mountain nights not to worry about her out there in the dark alone. But she seemed not to mind it or be frightened by it. In fact, she didn't seem to be frightened of much of anything but him.

He discarded his clothes and climbed inside his sleeping bag, looking for warmth. He had tried to leave her alone that afternoon and evening, and it had been difficult. He wanted her and he had never been very good at hiding the fact when he wanted a woman. But this was different. He couldn't help but feel that she was a woman who couldn't be rushed, a woman who needed a man beside her but one who wouldn't cover her shadow. In an almost desperate way she seemed to need the wind blowing around her, keeping her separate and whole.

He closed his eyes and tried to even out his breathing, forcefully holding his needs at bay. It was a trial that Greg Fisher was not accustomed to enduring.

He was just about asleep when the snap of a twig startled him wide awake. He opened his eyes and saw her standing beside him, naked except for the down bedroll that was draped across her shoulders and wrapped around her. In the moonlight, she was like a vision, a fantastic dream that was too good to be true. She was thick brown hair that hung loose over her shoulders. She was a white breast, a pale thigh, a bare forearm. And she was a clenched fist holding the blanket and her independence firmly in place.

Anne looked down at him and thought, *I know what I'm doing. This is the only way. I'm going to get him out of my system and this is the only way. It's the curiosity that's killing me, the wondering what it would be like with him. I'm going to find out and then it will be all over and I can regain my sanity.*

Greg stared up at her, thinking that women always came to him, flocked around him. It had always been that way. They couldn't stay away. This was nothing different. She was like all the rest. And yet he knew from the moment he had laid eyes on Anne Holdenfield that she was like no other woman he had ever met.

He carefully unzipped his sleeping bag and folded it back. Hers dropped from her shoulders and she knelt down beside him. Propped up on one elbow, he reached for her down cover on the ground, pulling it back around her protectively even as he pulled her down into his arms and the warmth of his bed.

"Hi," he whispered, still supporting himself on an elbow, with her lying beside him. One of his legs came up over hers, his knee resting between her thighs. "Glad you could join me." He smiled down into her tense face. "Now we can huddle together for warmth."

"Are you going to talk all the way through this the way you do everything else?"

"Not if you don't want me to."

Why does he care what I want, Anne wondered. Why didn't he just answer her simple question? Why didn't they just get on with this so she could confirm her suspicions about him? He was a man who treated women as appendages, who thought of them as pirate's plunder. He would be no different in lovemaking. It would be his show, with him reaping the benefits and the applause. She already knew this, so why didn't he just get on with it?

Her sigh was one of resignation. "Do you have any idea what you do to me?" she breathed in a tone that was half self-disgust, half molten desire.

With his hands supporting her bare back, he pulled her soft body up closer to his warmth and spoke in a low voice. "One thing I've learned in the last couple of days is never to second-guess Anne Holdenfield." His face was close to hers, and he smiled down as his eyes traveled slowly across her face, down her slim pale neck and to the spot beneath her breasts where their skin met. "So why don't you tell me. What do I do to you?"

"You'd like that, wouldn't you? You want to hear all sorts of wonderful things about yourself."

His slow grin was sheepish. "It's better than the alternative, I have to admit." He ran his thumb across her lower lip and a new charge of electricity coiled tightly within her abdomen. "Hey, don't look so glum. This is supposed to be fun." His mouth replaced his thumb on her lips in a quick, gentle kiss.

"You're doing this on purpose, aren't you?"

"What's that?"

"Taking your time. Going so slow."

He laughed at that. "Are we late for some appointment or something? We have all night, Anne. Why do you want me to rush it?" He regarded her closely and then nodded. "Ah, I get it. You don't like the fact that you're here in this sleeping bag with me, do you? You don't like the fact that you have normal sexual desires, that you have them for me. You're

trying so hard to deny that there is something between us.''

"Something physical," she clarified. *Nothing
more, Greg Fisher.*

"Okay, something physical. I want to make love to
you, Anne. Lying this close to me, I'm sure you're
aware of that. Don't look so embarrassed," he
chided, holding her face still beneath him. "You want
to make love to me, too. So what's wrong with that?
I'm not asking for some long-term commitment and
neither are you." The statement came from him as
easily as it alway had, and yet this time the words hung
like a sharp fish bone in his throat, a nagging, irritating thread of doubt.... She wasn't like other women
he had done this with. She wasn't like the others he
had said that to. She was not a one-night stand. This
was not just one more meaningless charade. This was
something special. She was special. A gift that must
be handled very, very carefully.

"Just a night of fun," she said bitterly, unaware of
the mass of bewildering thoughts that were swirling
through his head at that moment.

"I didn't say that," he answered roughly, and her
eyes widened at the brusque tone. He took a deep
breath and stared down into her dark brown eyes,
softening his voice. "You're different, Anne Holdenfield. You are a whole new species."

"You can add my name as a footnote to your file—
which is already extensive, I'm sure."

"You sound jealous."

"I just don't like being one of a long line of many."

"Maybe you're a whole new chapter," he suggested softly, stroking her lips once again with his thumb. His fingers began a slow exploratory caress of her face, her forehead, her eyes, cheeks, the bridge of her nose, her mouth and chin. "Did you ever think of that?"

Her eyes closed automatically as she succumbed to the hypnotic stroke of his fingers, the warm stroke of his voice. "Why am I here with you?" she asked in a last-ditch effort to understand the complexities of her feelings for him.

His hand slid ever so slowly to her breast, and his mouth lowered over it. "Because you want to be here," he whispered against her skin, and she felt a rush of liquid fire surge throughout her body. She stared up into the dark trees above them and felt a wonder unlike any she had felt before. *You're right,* she thought to herself. *I do want to be here.*

Her arms came around him, her hands against the back of his head, and her fingers gathered handfuls of his hair.

"You're so soft," he whispered. "And you taste so fresh."

"Thank you," she murmured, not having the faintest idea what she was saying.

He stopped and looked up at her. "You're welcome," he said, smiling, before dropping his head back to her breast. His mouth moved up to her neck, tasting every line and hollow, then moved back to her other breast and then lower still across her stomach, his hair still clutched in her fingers as his mouth trailed lower and lower across her body.

At that point, all murmurings were lost in the tide that slowly edged over her, his hands lapping like gentle waves against the waiting beach of her body. She had never felt like this before, never known the slow and exquisite pleasure a man's touch could bring. And she wanted to return the pleasure. She touched him as intimately as he was touching her and she felt him move against her, with her, his hands and his tongue and his hips filling her with a warmth that curled like golden flames of fire.

Her moans were muffled against his chest until he covered her mouth with his own, drinking in the ecstasy that she sighed with every breath. She loved the texture of his skin where it touched hers. He was rough where she was smooth, he was hard where she was yielding, he was thrusting where she was moist and receptive. And she relinquished herself to his control over her mind and her body and her entire being.

THE MOON WAS STRAIGHT OVERHEAD, casting its white light on the mountains. Greg lay with his arm around Anne, her head resting on his chest, her eyes closed in peace at last. She had not wanted to be with him. And yet she had given so much of herself to him. But even more than that, she had taken. He liked that about her. She wasn't willing to only give and not receive. She took pleasure in everything he could give her, the touch of his hands, the warmth of his mouth, the feel of his body moving with hers against the unyielding earth beneath them. Even now his body reacted sharply to the memory of their movements with and against each other. She had been so warm, so moist, so receptive.

That afternoon he had told her that looking for a mate was a universal quest. Until after he said it, he hadn't realized the truth of it. Everybody was looking for someone. Even Anne Holdenfield. Even Greg Fisher. He had always thought he was out strictly for a good time, a few laughs, and hopefully some sexual gratification along the way. But those moments had always been so fleeting. He knew that. He had even admitted that to himself many times. He just hadn't wanted to pursue it long enough to accept it as absolute truth. The girls and women he had known, both platonically and intimately, had left few indentations on his life. They came and went, and there were always more where they came from, always new faces, new bodies, new places to go. Until finally you realized that where you were going was where you had been and that all along you had been moving in circles, treading shallow, lifeless water in essentially the same spot.

Anne Holdenfield was the first woman he had ever known who stood outside the circle. She offered a challenge that had been missing in his life, a chance at something new, something on a somewhat straighter path, offering a haven and a boundary to his life. Yet at the same time there was something less confining than the narrow tunnel within which he had been existing.

Anne Holdenfield was indeed a rare bird, one he wasn't quite sure what to do with, but one that he was beginning to realize he did not want to do without. He pressed his lips against her hair and pulled her closer to him, and with the canopy of stars above them and the smoldering embers of the fire snapping beside them, they slept.

THE DAY WAS A SOFT PINK GLOW that radiated beyond the mountain peaks. Anne lay within the warmth of the sleeping bag she shared with Greg and watched the new day unfurl from the clutches of darkness. She turned her head and studied the man sleeping next to her. His sandy hair was mussed and his cheeks and chin were dark with the stubble he had not bothered to shave since coming to the mountains. He looked different with it, older than he had looked that first day standing outside her trailer like a lost, wet puppy. On that day she had known instinctively that he was a threat, but she had not known how serious a threat he would become. Then she had thought only of her peace and quiet, of his invasion of a solitude she protected and defended with almost ferocious intensity. It had not, on that day, entered her mind that she would have to defend herself against a whole different type of invasion from him. Even now she found it all so difficult to accept. She had taken him on this trip to the mine in the hope of getting rid of him. And then last night, when she could stay away from him no longer, her purpose had been essentially the same: to rid him from her thoughts for good.

It hadn't worked. The whole night had turned out so differently than she planned. Greg Fisher was so different from what she had expected. She had been positive that he would behave in lovemaking the same way he did in everything else—like an overgrown kid in a candy shop, with no regard for anything or anyone but himself, haphazardly tasting of the sweets, discarding what didn't suit his fancy, recklessly devouring what did. But she had been wrong.

She had been so wrong. He had been patient and slow and warm and gentle and caring, all attributes that she had assumed were missing in the man, all things she had never known with any other man. He hadn't gone into the storehouse of her body and grabbed all the merchandise for himself. He had taken, yes, but selectively, carefully, replenishing the supply as he moved them both with calculated ease to the same point of ecstasy.

Such an unforeseen surprise. And one that she had no idea what she was going to do with now. Her plan had been so simple, but no more. Now nothing was simple at all.

Very slowly, so as not to wake him, she slid out of the bedroll and hurriedly dressed in the chill air. She walked to the nearby spring and washed her face in the icy water, then filled the coffeepot and headed back to the campsite to start a fire for breakfast. She wondered where Solomon and his ewe were today. Maybe if they got an early start they could find them. Besides, they would need to move right out because they were still at least two days away from the location Greg had pinpointed on his map as the site of the mine.

She built the fire and hooked the kettle of water over a branch to heat, then walked over to the sleeping man and stuck out her foot to nudge him awake. But before her toe met the sleeping bag, he reached out and grabbed her ankle, yanking it so she lost her balance, careened backward and toppled to the ground. In a split second he was out of the bedroll and on top of her.

"Thought you were going to get away with that again, didn't you?" Greg said into her startled, breathless face, laughter in his voice and his eyes.

The wind had been knocked out of her and she struggled for breath. "What are you doing!" she cried, wiggling to get out from beneath him.

He held her fast and captured her mouth with his. "Saying good morning," he murmured against her neck, his voice and body and kisses as full of life as the sap of a new spring tree.

A jellylike weakness flooded through her body, a thrill of physical pleasure that surprised her with its force. This man had the unique ability to make her feel soft and yielding and totally feminine and yet also allow her to remain separate from him, to retain some sense of independence. It was the first time any man had ever made her feel that way. Always before it had been one or the other. An equal, platonic partner or a subservient slave of a man's desires.

"What am I going to do with you, Greg Fisher?" she said with a sigh, knowing that whatever the choice it wasn't going to be easy.

"Let me count the ways," he said with a leer, laughing at her flushed cheeks. "I can't believe it, Anne Holdenfield blushing! This is an anomaly that we must include in your scientific journal."

"I am not blushing," she replied hotly.

"No?"

"Absolutely not. I'm just suffocating beneath you, that's all."

He tried not to smile. "Oh, I see." Rolling over, he pulled her on top of him. He was totally naked while she was dressed in denim and flannel and hiking boots. "You like this better?"

She struggled out of his arms. "Don't be fatuous, Greg."

Propping himself up on one elbow, he watched her walk over to the fire and stoop down to remove the boiling kettle of water. "I'm not trying to be fatuous," he said seriously. "I'm just trying to understand Anne Holdenfield and what it is she wants."

She looked over at him, taking in the bare length of his body, the body that had made her cry out in utter abandon beneath him last night. She smiled weakly. "If she finds out, you'll be the first to know."

He studied her for a long moment. "Guess I can't ask for much more than that, can I?"

She walked over to him and knelt down, tentatively touching his hair with her fingertips. "No, you can't. And I don't want you to expect too much from me, Greg Fisher. I don't have a lot to give."

His smile was slow and gentle. "I think you have no idea how much you have. I've just touched the surface, and I'll be willing to bet there's a whole untapped vein of gold in you just waiting to be discovered."

Her face grew still and serious. "You're the gambler. I've done all the playing with odds I ever intend to do in my life. So if you're looking for a good gamble, you've picked the wrong track. This one closed down a long time ago.''

Chapter Nine

A light drizzle began around nine o'clock but only lasted for a few minutes. The clouds moved on, the sky cleared and the day grew warm and fragrant. For breakfast they had cooked cereal and coffee, and Greg's stomach began its midmorning complaint within an hour after it. He cured the pain with a giant-size Milky Way, offering half of it to Anne, who turned down the overture with barely restrained disgust.

They hiked through a large green basin where they saw a couple of deer grazing on the slope at the edge of a line of trees where the matted leathery kinnikinnick plant grew in the moisture and the shade. "Do you think we'll see any elk?" Greg asked.

"It's possible," Anne answered. "But they are more difficult to get within range of than deer. They react differently to approaching danger. Deer tend to wait until you're very close before they get scared, then they'll bound off for a short distance, stop and look back at you, and then settle down to feed again. Elk, on the other hand, will watch you approach for a while, and then when you get within what they consider threatening range, they will take off and they won't stop until they are miles away. Once they leave, you won't see them again.''

The fields were alive with brilliant color as they trudged through them, and Anne could name the almost endless variety of flowers. There was mountain bluebell, primrose, wild licorice, monkshood and a plant called fireweed, which she claimed was adored by grizzly bears.

Greg's voice was cautiously curious. "Are there any around here?''

"Grizzlies?'' she asked, laughing at his anxious glance toward the dark shadows that waved among the trees. "No, there aren't any grizzlies left in Colorado. Quite a few brown bears, though. Be on the lookout; we may just be lucky enough to see one.''

"Lucky enough, he repeated, positive now that this woman was nuts. ''That kind of luck I can do without.'' He pointed toward a nearby treetop. ''Is that a hummingbird up there?''

"Yes.'' They stopped and watched the tiny bird dive toward the meadow and flutter its wings as it hung suspended in the air, drinking the sweet nectar from a flower.

They forded a rapidly flowing creek by hopping from one huge boulder to the next and found themselves on the other side in a field of Indian paintbrush ranging in color from pale yellowish white to a deep blood rose.

"Where did you grow up?'' she asked, after almost an hour of silence.

Greg caught up with her and walked beside her. "All over, really. My dad was a military man, a major in the air force."

"A military brat." She smiled to herself. "Did you live overseas?"

"Yeah, for a while we lived in Germany. Before that we were in Japan. I was born in Tokyo. And then we lived in a lot of different places in the states. Omaha, San Antonio, even Colorado Springs for a few months, but I was young then so I don't remember too much about it."

"Wasn't that hard, moving around so much?" she asked, understanding for the first time what had formed his outgoing personality. To move from one place to another, to make new friends over and over again, one would have to develop skills for fitting in easily.

"Sure, sometimes," he said. "I had to learn to make friends easily. Although I don't remember ever having any really close friends until I was in college."

That, too, could explain his flitting from one relationship to another. He learned at a very young age that friendship and relationships just don't last for very long. "What about your mother?" Anne asked. "What was she like?"

"Oh, she was what I would call your typical officer's wife. She attended all the right luncheons and meetings and parties. She did all the 'right' things. We were never extremely close. She was very social, always in the middle of activities." He shrugged. "But she was a nice woman. She had lots of friends, and everyone seemed to genuinely like her."

Anne was quiet for a while, thinking about Greg's mother and father and how they must have greatly influenced his views on male-female roles. Parents always do. Whether they realize it or not, they set the pattern for their children's lives.

He offered nothing more about his family and she decided not to delve too deeply.

A camaraderie of sorts had developed between them, and it made this morning much more pleasant than the previous ones had been. There were still isolated displays of physical superiority on her part, as well as her inevitable impatience, and Greg continued to find something funny in even the most serious of subjects, as well as to complain about the weight of the backpack that amazingly enough had not seemed to grow one ounce lighter as the days progressed. Nor did he cease making his hunger or sore feet or shortness of breath known to every living creature around them. Still, it was easier between them, looser somehow and definitely warmer.

Anne found herself talking to him more about himself, about his career and his students.

"I do enjoy teaching," he admitted. "It's just that sometimes I look out over that huge classroom and all I see are fifty pairs of zombie eyes staring back at me. That's what really bothers me. It's when I know I've lost them and when I know that nothing I say that day is going to bring them back. That's the hard part."

"But I know it's not always that way," she insisted. "If you explain history to them the way you explained that lost mine to me, they would have to be interested.''

"I suppose most of the time I have them on the hook. They can ask some fairly probing questions occasionally and I of course give brilliant answers to them all."

Anne smiled to herself. "Of course."

"What I mainly try to teach these kids is that history is an ongoing thing, a constantly evolving process. I try to get them involved in present-day events that will be embedded in history tomorrow. For example, if you attend a political rally where the president or vice president is, then you're living history."

Anne sniffed. "I attended one once. It wasn't living history, it was living hell. I thought I was going to pass out from the heat and the crowd. Still," she said, shrugging, "I get your point." She pursed her lips and murmured, "Probably better than you intend for me to."

He looked over at her. "What is that supposed to mean?"

She shrugged again. "Oh, you know, living to the fullest in the present because tomorrow this will all be history."

His mouth tightened into a thin line. "I didn't say that."

"There's nothing wrong with it," she said too brightly. "Nothing wrong with making the most of the present, of living for the moment." She smiled at him, working hard to adopt a thoroughly modern, independent expression. After all, she was an intelligent woman. She could accept the fact that after these few days she would never see him again. Yes, she could accept that.

She looked away from him and back down at the deer trail they were now following through the forest. And the question that loomed up in her mind was "How?"

For their lunch they stopped just below a beaver dam where a thin stream escaped the lodge and still ran through a lush meadow of willow and aspen. They had grilled some freeze-dried meat patties that morning over the breakfast fire, so they had those and some dried apricots and raisins.

"I can't wait to have a thick juicy cheeseburger again," Greg moaned. "How can you stand eating like this all summer?"

"You get used to it," she said. "Actually, I've learned to fix some delicious meals at my trailer. Lots of plants around here make wonderful soups and herbs for stews. And there are always good berries to eat. Why are you shaking your head?"

He was doing just that. "You amaze me, that's all."

"Why?"

"I don't know. I guess it's the fact that you live up here all alone for entire summers. It's unusual enough for anyone, but especially for a woman. I guess...in a way I suppose I'm a little envious of your ability to do it. I don't think I could. I really don't think I could stay up here all by myself that long. I need people and human stimuli too much."

"We're different," she said, reiterating that fact to herself as much as to him.

He knew exactly what she was doing. And she was right. They were different; their lives had taken completely opposite tracks. Maybe it was that very difference that drew them together, making those tracks intersect for a little while before once again splitting apart to follow their own courses.

"Is that why your marriage didn't work?" he asked, watching her closely as she nibbled on a raisin.

She sighed. "It was a lot of things, but that wasn't one of them. Actually we were very much alike. Frank liked the outdoors. He had a genuine respect for the environment. He was an extremely intelligent man, independent, warm, caring…"

"He sounds too good to have gotten rid of."

Anne pulled at the thin grasses beside her. "Well, I'm sure it was my fault."

"Oh, come on," he scoffed. "It takes two to tango."

She looked over at him and laughed. "Funny, I don't remember ever dancing with Frank—the tango or anything else." She smiled a bit wistfully. "Truly, though, I'm not the easiest person to get along with."

Greg did a good imitation of shock. "No!"

"I'm stubborn, as you well know. I don't take orders well from anyone. I expected our marriage to be more of a partnership than it was."

"You mean he wasn't a liberated male?"

"Don't make jokes, Greg. It wasn't funny at the time and it still isn't. I was never able to be the woman he wanted me to be." She paused thoughtfully. "I was never really sure what he wanted. I thought he wanted an equal, so I tried to be that. But despite what he professed to want in me, he didn't really want it. He dominated me with an iron thumb. Men don't really want women to be their equals, do they, Greg? Even if they say so, they really don't.''

"Men like to wear the pants in a family," he said flippantly, but only because he couldn't reconcile his own change in opinion on that. Three days ago he would have believed it wholeheartedly. But now, after being with a woman who was his equal and in many cases his superior, he just wasn't sure what was important anymore. For the first time in his life, he found himself on an equal footing with a woman. Not necessarily above or below, but on a relatively even plane. There was something quite satisfactory about it. Something nonthreatening and secure. But it was such a new experience for him that he wasn't sure how to put it into words.

Glancing at her face now, he knew he had done nothing to reassure her or change her opinions about men. The moment to do so was gone and he had lost his chance.

At that moment a flutter in the bushes caught their attention and from the top of a tree an eagle took flight, gliding on the air currents, soaring over the treetops above them.

"Is that an eagle?" he asked.

"Yes, a golden eagle," Anne said. "They're such beautiful birds."

They watched until the bird was out of sight, crossing in minutes what it would take them hours or even days to cross.

They climbed up out of the timber that afternoon, heading toward the upper edge of the subalpine zone. Cold winds up that high restricted the growth of trees and they became dwarfed, their trunks lying at odd angles along the ground, their leaves joined in a protective canopy that reached three or four feet high.

As Anne and Greg climbed, the air became thinner and colder. Low grasses and rock fields made up the base of the alpine tundra, but a rich display of flowers bloomed in profusion among the rocks. There were bright yellow buttercups, forget-me-nots, mustard, strawberries and asters, all in a rainbow of reds, blues, pinks, whites, yellows and purples. The tightly matted sedge that covered the ground beneath the flowers provided food and cover for squirrels and mice and voles, and good grazing for the bighorn sheep and elk and deer that spent their summers at these high elevations. There were isolated patches of snow and ice that they had to traverse, and above this tundra was the line of perpetual snow.

Anne stopped to readjust her pack and catch her breath, while Greg had to fight to retain his balance. He had never felt so dizzy in his life.

"You okay?" she asked, frowning when she noticed how pale he had become.

"Wonderful," he answered a little too brightly, bending over on the pretext of pulling up his socks.

"Are you going to faint?" she asked, seeing right through his act.

He lifted up slowly and took in a slow, even breath, expelling it even slower. "No. Whoo! I'm fine now, really I am."

"It's the altitude," she said. "I'm surprised it hasn't affected you before now."

He puffed out his chest and gloated, "See, I'm not in such bad shape."

"Yes," she mumbled under her breath, "and I know now what you do to keep in shape."

He feigned shock at that, but let it pass.

Anne turned away and once again lifted her binoculars to her eyes and scanned the ruts and furrows beneath them.

"You don't see him?"

She shook her head, disappointment etched in the afternoon shadows that fell across her face.

They had seen a herd of sheep earlier in the morning and had crouched down on a ledge to watch them graze, but they still hadn't seen Solomon or the ewe he had found to mate with.

"We'll be turning south," she said. "They were heading west, so we probably won't see them again."

He walked over next to her and stopped. "I'm sorry, Anne. I've taken you away from your research."

She studied his face for a long moment, coming to the conclusion that he really was sincere. Still, it didn't change the fact that he needed her help and would not take kindly to her leaving him here to find his own way.

She retied her pack strap around her waist and started walking again. "What are you going to do with the money if you win this bet?"

She had asked him that before, but he had been vague at best. This time he was honest. "I have some bad debts to pay off.'' He shrugged at her glance. ''I told you, I'm a gambler.''

''Compulsive?''

He looked startled at her worried expression. He had never really thought about that before. ''No,'' he scoffed. ''At least I don't think so.'' He shook his head more firmly this time. ''No, I'm sure of it.''

''Then why do you do it?''

He was quiet for a minute while he thought about that one. He had avoided introspection at all costs. He didn't want to examine the inner workings of Greg Fisher. He had always liked himself the way he was and he didn't want to find out that there were things about him that might be less than likable. ''Bored, I think,'' he finally said, surprised by the admission. ''When the school day is over, I have no place I have to go, no one I have to go home to. If I wanted to I could give the same class lectures over year after year, so there isn't much work I have to do. Gambling is the only challenge I have in my life.'' He studied her for a moment. ''You have disapproval in your eyes.''

''I do?''

''Heavy disdain is a better term for it.''

She shrugged it away. ''Who am I to disapprove of you?''

''But you do. Why?''

She looked away. ''Oh, this is silly, Greg. I have no right to tell—''

''Is it the drinking?'' he interrupted. ''The gambling? The other women?''

''I really don't want to talk about this,'' she insisted, her chin raised high and proud.

"Why not?"

"Because it doesn't concern me."

He stared hard at her, weighing her words and her expression. Okay, he could play the game, too. He had been playing games for thirty-six years. "You're right," he finally said. "It doesn't concern you."

Her chin lifted even higher. "Subject closed, then?"

"Subject closed."

AFTER THEIR DINNER THAT EVENING, Greg washed the metal dishes and cups in a stream and packed up the cache of food, hanging it high in a tree beyond the reach of predators. Anne had gone for a walk among the trees, and he was left alone to tend the fire. He sat on a log and picked up a stick, stirring the embers with it. As his eyes scanned the campsite, they landed on her pack propped against the trunk of a tall fir. Lying on the ground beside it was her journal.

He stared at it for a minute, then looked back at the fire. But his eyes were drawn back to the notebook time and time again. Finally he dropped the stick, stood up and walked over to the tree. He looked into the forest where Anne had gone; then he bent over and picked up the journal. He carried it over to the fire and sat back down on the log. Opening it, he read the instructions for her study from one Dr. Willoughby Knight.

"The purpose of this study," Dr. Knight stated, "is to immerse the biologist in her chosen environment for an extended period of time, and to record her observations on the natural phenomena around her and to evaluate her own responses to life in a hostile environment. In addition, she is to monitor the behavior of one particular species of animal as it relates to the changing conditions and to its own migratory cycles.''

Greg turned to Anne's first entry. ''May 28. The trip here was smooth. The Forest Service helicopter dropped me and my supplies near the trailer this morning and I have spent the day getting organized. Tomorrow I will. . .'' He flipped over each page until he came to the one dated June 13. The day he arrived at her doorstep. To his surprise, there was no mention of him. He had been right. Dishonest or not, she had thought that by not mentioning him in her journal, she could ignore the fact that he was there.

He flipped to the next page. ''June 14. Today I went to Evan's Park and watched the herd of sheep. They were placid and seemed not to notice my presence....'' Greg skipped through the details of her day, searching for a reference to him. He found it at the bottom of the page. ''I had a visitor yesterday. He has camped no more than fifty feet away and seems to have no intention of moving on. If I ignore him perhaps he will leave.'' And then, with an enigmatic close to the day's entry, it read, ''Perhaps not.''

He scanned the following day and the mention of him was brief and to the point. ''That obnoxious man is still here, stinking up the air with his cigarette smoke and frightening the animals with his bawdy tavern ditties. He must go!''

The next day the entry was decidedly lopsided in favor of him. There were only a couple of paragraphs about the ram they had spotted in the gulch below them and there was half a page about Greg Fisher. "He complains incessantly," she wrote. "And he smokes too much, and talks too much, and I don't know how much longer I can put up with him. He is interesting in some ways—ways I cannot yet put my finger on. There is a boyish quality about him, a sense of adventure and fun that few men his age would dare admit to having. And I also have to admit that he makes me laugh. I can't remember the last time I've smiled or laughed as much. But I do wish we would hurry and find this mine so that he could go back where he belongs and I could once again be left with my world intact. He said some things tonight in our camp that bother me. He called me a tyrant. I haven't thought of myself as that since that night three years ago when Frank called me a...well, I can't even write the word Frank used. This man Fisher also claims that I have not smiled in three days. But that is not true. I already wrote that I hadn't remembered smiling so much for years. He also told me I appeared not to be afraid of anything. This man does strange things to me. I can't wait until he is gone."

He was reading faster now and he noticed very little in her journal about the environment or about animals living in the wild, or anything she was supposed to be writing about. It was more and more about him.

"He told me I was pretty when I smiled," she wrote in the next day's entry. "He asked me if I don't get lonely for a man. How can I tell him that I have learned the hard way that I am not meant to have relationships with men? How can I tell him that I have never been truly fulfilled in passion or in love? How can I tell him about the hurt I have known? Love is something I am not destined to know. But how this intriguing man from Princeton tempts me!''

And the last entry. ''June 17. I think I have made a grave error. A disastrous mistake. I had thought by sleeping with him I could rid myself of this man's charm. During the day I grew to like him. For the first time I could actually say I liked him. But last night I took it too far. I didn't want to feel anything for Greg Fisher. I didn't think I could ever feel the way he makes me feel. I'm not sure I will like the feeling at all when he is gone.''

ANNE WALKED BACK into the campsite and stopped a few feet away from Greg. He was sitting on a log with his forearms resting on his thighs. His profile was grim. His eyes were directed on the fire.

At his feet was her journal.

He looked up and in the light of the campfire saw the wariness in her eyes.

''You weren't even going to try and hide the fact, were you?'' Her voice was soft but accusatory. ''You didn't even put it back where you found it and pretend that you hadn't read it.''

''I'm not that kind of person,'' he said evenly. ''I'm not dishonest.''

''Reading someone else's journal is hardly the most ethical thing to do.''

''I didn't know that...I hadn't realized that it would deal with anything...quite so personal.''

She bent down and picked it up from the dirt at his feet, dusted it off and held it against her breast. Turning away, she walked over to her pack and slipped it inside the back pocket.

She hadn't known that he was following her, but when she turned around he was there, his arms enclosing her, his mouth against her hair.

"I don't need this in my life," she said, softly crying against his chest. "I don't want you here."

"I know," he murmured against her neck while his hands moved like waves along her back and down across her hips. His lips trailed up her neck and over her chin toward her waiting mouth.

"I'll be glad when you're gone," she whispered as his lips met hers in a duel of longing and withdrawal, of hunger and self-denial.

"Yes," he breathed, pulling her to the ground with him, "I know."

She was swept away with the stroke of his fingers as he unbuttoned her shirt and ran his hands over the thin nylon material beneath. "But do you also know—"

"Yes," he whispered, lowering his face to the lacy camisole, taking it and her breast into his mouth.

Her hands moved up under his shirt, her fingers dug into his back and pulled him more tightly against her. Nothing mattered in that moment, nothing mattered in life but the feel of his hands as they lowered the zipper on her jeans and caressed her, lifting her, making her a part of him and him a part of her.

She had been waiting for him, waiting for this all her life. But no man had ever been able to give her what she needed and wanted. Only Greg Fisher. Only this man from a world far removed from her own, a man so different in basic philosophy that she would never have dreamed of falling in love with him. And yet he was a man whose touch could take her to places she never dreamt of going.

His hands were everywhere, his fingers probing the moist recesses of her body, his mouth exploring hers in a way no man had ever dared. His kisses trailed like fire across her flesh, bringing her to life, carrying her on the spreading wings of passion. Her cries mingled with the night sounds, her moans collided with his, her murmured words of love lost in whispers of passion that burned on his lips.

And when he moved inside her, her body expanded to absorb him, to hold him in, to be filled by the hot essence of him and to become one in the flesh and the mind with this man she had vowed to resist, with this man who had buried himself in the very core of her life.

Later, as they lay wrapped together in the soft matted bear grass, Anne shivered in his arms.

"Cold?" he asked, holding her more tightly.

"Freezing."

"How about getting even colder still?"

She turned toward him and frowned. "What do you mean?"

"Let's go take a bath together...in the stream, the way you did that first night. I've yet to brave it at night."

"Can you handle it?" she said, smiling.

"I'll give it the old college try."

He helped her up, and together they walked hand in hand to the fast-moving creek. The water was frigid and the rocks were slippery and cold.

"Here, hold on," he said, as they gingerly made their way into the bubbling stream. "Our own Jacuzzi."

"Where's the heat?" she cried.

"I thought you liked this sort of thing. The rugged life and all that."

She shivered again. "I just changed my mind. And how come you're not complaining about it? You complain about everything."

"I don't!"

"You most certainly do."

"Come here, wench," he said, grabbing her and pulling her into the tumbling water. "And don't scream in my ear. Ouch! Don't bite my ear, either."

With her arms around his neck, they frolicked and played in the icy creek, like children who were having far too much fun to admit that they were miserably cold.

"Hey," he said, "what shall we name Solomon's old lady?"

"I've already named her," Anne said, splashing water on his face. "Sheba."

He dodged the spray of water. "Solomon and Sheba. Not bad. Why didn't I think of that?"

"Because I thought of it first."

"You think you're real smart, don't you?" He dunked her under the water. "Don't you?"

"Smarter than you," she cried, wriggling out of his arms and making her way to the bank.

"Hey, where are you going?" he called after her.

She laughed over her shoulder. "I'm going to see how brave you are. We're going to see how long you can stay down here at the creek...in the dark...by yourself."

"No problem," he huffed. "I'm not afraid of anything."

Her laughter trailed behind her as she ran back to the camp and the warmth of the fire.

Greg crawled out on the bank and sat down, shivering like a half-drowned cat. "I'm not afraid of anything," he grumbled to himself. "Nothing. Thinks she's so damn smart. I'll show her...."

At that moment the most terrifying noise he had ever heard echoed in the air above him, accompanied by a huge black fluttering that crashed into the willow bushes, smashing, hacking, screaming.

He took off for the campsite and made it in half the time it took Anne. "It's a bear!" he cried. "Or a wolf! Did you hear it? It's alive! It's coming to get us!"

Anne's hysterical laughter bounded off the canyon walls that surrounded them as she stared at Greg, stark naked and dripping wet before her, with panic written in every line of his face.

"I heard it, Greg," she said, laughing so hard her sides ached. "It was an owl."

He stared at her while the water ran in rivulets down his face and bare chest. "An owl?"

"Yes," she replied, her laughter now down to a giggle. "An owl."

"Oh," he said, walking over to his backpack to pull out a towel. "I knew that. Knew it all the time."

Her warm, rich laughter followed him until he stalked over to her and silenced her once more when his mouth claimed hers for the night.

Chapter Ten

In a way, Anne knew that their relationship was much like that of the miners who came to the Rocky Mountains in the second half of the nineteenth century. The roots of those men went only as deep as the high-grade ore they dug and panned for. When that played out, the miners moved on. That was the way it would be with Greg. They had found a physical bond, but it wouldn't hold them together for long. She guessed that he was a restless man, driven to explore and find new territories, never allowing his roots to grow too deep in one spot. He had settled with her—but only for a short while. She was a new bonanza, a new prosperous vein, but like the miners before him, he no doubt saw the virgin frontier as endless, wide open for his exploration and plunder.

Anne realized all this about him and she accepted it. She had known from the beginning that their relationship could not last. They were too different from each other. They did not want or need the same things in life.

But as much as her rational mind told her this, as much as she convinced herself that it was so, it did not ease her dread of the end. As the days passed, the day when they would part hurled closer and closer and, with a kind of desperation, she wanted to hold on to the present and drag it out for as long as she could.

They spent the following day climbing still higher, up along the band of tundra that separated the forested slopes from the peaks of perpetual snow. They traversed the rocky knolls, working their way up the jagged escarpments and jutting spine of America's great watershed, the Continental Divide, where some sixty-five million years ago folds of old sediment were pushed upward by the great fiery forces within the earth.

Up here, Greg finally understood the awe that Anne had spoken of the other day. It seemed as if he could see forever, as if the earth lay like a jagged and buckled carpet beneath him. It gave him the sensation of omnipotence and at the same time made him feel less significant than the tiny alpine buttercups that bloomed profusely in bright yellow clumps at their feet.

"I think I finally understand," he said almost reverently.

"What?" she asked, turning around to let him catch up with her.

"I see now why you must live up here in the summers. It's...it almost defies emotional description, doesn't it?"

"Yes, it does. You know, I've been coming here for several years now and I still haven't accurately recorded the colors and the smells and the sounds of this place.''

His arm came around her shoulder, easily, as if it belonged there, as if it always had. They walked side by side this way and her arm circled his waist, wanting to hold him as near as she could until he had to go. They walked this way along the Great Divide, knowing that like the rainfall and the snowmelt along this ridge, they, too, would split and go in opposite directions.

They constructed a lean-to for the night to protect themselves against the strong prevailing winds. It took several hours and most of their energy just to set up camp, and after a hot meal of freeze-dried chicken mixed with noodles and a dessert of some dried dates, they fell asleep together in one sleeping bag.

The following day was just as hard. They crossed wide rock slides, forded creeks and picked their way across numerous icy snowbanks. They stopped frequently to rest and recheck their positions against the map. Anne had taught Greg how to use a compass properly and he was now able to contribute to the expedition as much as she. They both felt sure that they must be getting close to the spot he had marked on the map, but after going back and forth across the same terrain several times, they found no evidence of any mine. At the height of their discouragement and fatigue they noticed something they had missed before.

Anne had stopped and was looking up at the ridge above them. The formation of it and the way the rock stuck straight up in the air seemed odd to her. ''Greg, look up there," she said, pointing to the ridge. "Let's take a look at that."

They climbed up the rocks, pulling and pushing each other up the last few feet. Once there, they discovered a slim fissure in the side of the rocky slope, a narrow furrow that ran about fifty yards across and down at a forty-five-degree angle. The entrance was partially covered by scrubby, low-lying krummholz, and if they had not been paying close attention, they might have missed it altogether. They stopped and stared at each other.

"This is it, Anne," Greg said, pulling out the map and poring over it for at least the hundredth time. "It has to be."

Her voice echoed the excitement that was in his. "It would explain Stoneface Johnson's disappearance each time, wouldn't it? If they were below him, down there somewhere, he could have slipped through here and they never would have known where he went."

Greg looked down the rocks in the direction they had come. Then he looked back at the slim opening. "From down there, it would look as if he just disappeared into thin air."

"Into the sky," she added, then touched his arm and smiled. "You know what? I think you're going to win your ten-thousand-dollar bet."

His eyes flared with barely contained excitement and he grabbed hold of her arms. "Do you realize what I can do with all that money? Do you have any idea?"

She knew she should feel happy for him. She knew she should want him to win the bet. But the excitement that was lit up inside him now had nothing at all to do with her, and she couldn't control the resentment she felt. "I suppose it would buy a lot of friendly nights, wouldn't it?" she mumbled sarcastically.

He frowned at her for a second, puzzling over her remark. "Right," he finally said, concentrating more on what lay on the other side of that crevasse than on what his winning of the bet could mean to her or their relationship. "Let's try it, okay?"

"Okay," she said, trying to muster up enthusiasm for his sake. "I'm ready." She felt his hand on her arm and she turned around. His brilliant blue eyes were intense and shiny as they bore into hers. He ran both hands up and down the length of her arms, and she felt a longing for him that went far beyond the physical.

"I just want to thank you, Anne. Even if this isn't it, even if we don't find the mine, you've done so much. I've taken you away from your work. I've driven you crazy and scared away your animals and interrupted your solitude.... You've sacrificed a lot for me."

If you only knew how much I've sacrificed, she thought, wanting to tell him exactly how much, but she kept the pain deep inside and only smiled thinly. "I want you to find your mine, Greg. I want you to have the satisfaction of winning your bet." It was not a total lie. Despite the resentment, despite the ache of losing him, she did want him to succeed and to win.

"I promised you fifteen hundred of it," he reminded her.

"I don't want your money. I told you that. I just wanted to make sure you didn't fall off the mountain."

He grinned. "Come on, now, be truthful. Those first few days you wanted nothing more than to push me off the highest cliff you could find."

She laughed softly. "You're right there. You were undoubtedly the biggest pest I've ever seen."

He wrapped his arms around her waist and pulled her close. "And now?"

She paused, forcing herself to swallow the truth that wanted to pour forth. "And now," she stated softly but firmly, "we're going to go through this hole in the sky and find your mine."

He sighed, half in disappointment and half in relief as he loosened his hold on her. "I'm ready if you are," he said, and they turned together and began working their way through the thick covering of dwarf trees that had survived this high altitude because of the rocky precipice that hung over them, protecting them from the fierce icy winds.

Once inside the hidden recess, they began the difficult climb down the tumbles of rocks that had broken loose from the hard granite and created this irregularity in the mountain. It was slow going, and they had to continually stop and find a handhold as their feet slipped along the loose rocks.

Greg was leading this time and he had to find the rocks that were steady enough to place their weight on. Fifty yards was not far on the flat straight and narrow. But in this terrain, it took almost an hour to make it through the fissure.

Greg came out of the opening at the other end first and stopped, staring around him in amazement. Anne came out shortly behind and stood beside him, her eyes wide and disbelieving as she took in the scene in front of her.

It was like a place forgotten by time. The very air carried a signature of another time, another place, of a world that had been etched out of the rock, yet had somehow survived to tell about it.

Almost completely surrounded by mountains, the circular area was sheltered from the harsh life above timberline and had the appearance of a montane that had been cleared of its trees. Delicate grasses grew among the tumble of old wooden structures and tinder-dry flanks. A cabin that had been tightly chinked with lime to insulate a previous resident was still intact, but its square-hewn logs were splintered and sagging with age. Clumps of wild hyacinth and phlox, larkspur and wild licorice bloomed amid the crumbling ruins.

"This couldn't be Johnson's mine," Greg marveled. "One man could not have done all of this."

They tried to take in the scene, noticing several large structures and pieces of equipment that had survived the years.

"They seem to have dug tunnels a long way back under that ridge." Anne pointed and Greg followed her gaze. There were ore buckets and hundreds of feet of cable that had been used to winch the buckets in and out of the tunnels.

Shafts had been dug and ribbed with heavy poles. As they moved closer to the shafts, they saw that the holes were now filled with water. A rusted ore cart sat eerily in a silent mine shaft. A tin plate, a crumpled boot, pieces of a rotting sluice box were all hidden among the fallen planks of wood and somehow had miraculously managed to escape the ravages of time.

"I can't believe this!" Anne marveled. "I just can't."

"I've got to get some pictures," Greg said, hurrying to remove his camera as if the scene would fade like a mirage before his eyes. "This can't be Pervis Johnson's mine, but whomever it belonged to, it was and is incredible."

He moved around the site taking photographs of everything, of light bars that flooded the interior of a small mill in a crazy-quilt pattern, of plank board-walks that went nowhere, of rusted pickheads, of weathered picket fences, of iron nails.

He bent down and pulled something from a clump of blue flowers.

"Is that a battery?" she asked, kneeling down beside him.

He nodded. "We're obviously not the first to find this place."

"Look at that!" she said, pointing to a mine shaft about thirty feet away. "That ore cart wasn't there in the nineteenth century! It's fairly new!"

They stepped over to the shaft of newly turned earth and Greg shook his head in frustration. "I thought we had found it. I thought this was Johnson's...." He walked away, kicking irritably at some rusted tools that lay in his path, and then rounded the corner of a badly listing clapboard cabin. He cut between two crumbling buildings and found himself in front of a narrow gate. He stepped through it and stopped dead in his tracks.

"Anne," he called. "Get over here!"

She hurried over to him, sidestepping the pieces of wood that had fallen helter-skelter about the place. "What is it?"

She stopped and stared with him at the row of wooden slabs that stuck up through the wild strawberries and geraniums. Tombstones, badly weathered and listing from age, stood as testament that men had been there—had been there and died.

Together they carefully picked their way through the grass and flowers to the first grave marker. They stooped down and dusted away the dirt and pollen that hung in the carved writing.

"It looks Oriental,' he said.

"Chinese, maybe."

They stood up and moved to the next one. It, too, had similar markings. And the next and the next, until they had covered the entire area. There were at least twenty wooden headstones, and all were in the same ideographic writing. Except for one. One marker stood apart from the others, with strange markings unlike the others.

In a kind of daze they stood side by side and surveyed the area. "There were a lot of Chinese who worked the mines back then."

Anne frowned as her eyes swept across the hidden valley. "It's not as if it was a town," she said. "I don't see the remains of a school or hotel or anything."

"Just the mine and a few cabins," he added in a tone of amazement that equaled her own.

At that moment, from nowhere, a shot rang out, bouncing and echoing against the sheer rock cliffs that surrounded them. Stunned at the loud noise and not knowing for sure what it was, they stood still, unable to move a muscle. A second shot was fired, and this time they realized that someone, somewhere up there, had a gun.

"Where did that come—" Another shot followed, and another, and the dirt at their feet scattered as bullets landed close by.

Anne screamed and Greg instinctively jumped in front of her as the volley of shots continued to ring out around them.

A sharp, vivid pain struck Greg's left arm and he reached to cover it with his right.

"You're hurt!" she cried, but Greg gave neither of them time to process that information. He spun her around with his right arm and together they dashed for the rock that held the only promise of escape. They darted between the long-abandoned cabins, around the remains of a small mill, trampling the grasses and flowers that had reclaimed the territory that was rightfully theirs.

Blood oozed between the fingers of Greg's right hand where they clutched his other arm, but the pain had not yet had a chance to reach his brain.

"Hurry!" he urged, pushing Anne ahead of him as they ran as fast as they could toward the opening in the rocks. They didn't stop to listen if the shots had ceased; they just kept running.

They reached the crevasse and Anne went through the narrow crack first, scrambling her way up the forty-five-degree angle across the slippery, loose rocks. Greg was right behind her, still holding his arm, the pain still at bay. Anne turned around once and looked worried. "Are you okay?" she asked.

"Don't stop, Anne! Keep moving."

She obeyed and turned around, using her hands to help her find the safest footing through the fissure in the rocks.

It was almost an hour of hard climbing before they reached the other side. Anne plopped down on a rock and took huge breaths, replacing the fear in her lungs with the fresh scent of pine and wildflowers. Greg sat down beside her and tried to catch his breath, too. Neither of them said anything for several minutes.

Anne was the first to speak. "What happened back there? Who was shooting at us, Greg?"

He shook his head, not yet having the oxygen to speak. He was light-headed and very dizzy, but he wasn't sure if it was from the altitude or the injury.

"Let me see your arm," she said, reaching for him. The fingers of his right hand were almost glued to the spot on his left arm where the blood was beginning to cake and dry.

"Careful," he said, as she pried his fingers and the material of his shirt loose.

"There's quite a bit of blood, Greg, but I can't tell how deep the wound is. Are you in a lot of pain?"

"Not really," he said, still stunned from the initial impact of the injury. "I just want us to get away from here. We need to get to some place safe."

Anne looked up at the threatening sky. Black clouds were rolling in and another thunderstorm was imminent. "Are you sure you can keep going?"

He stood up. "I'm sure."

She followed, and they began working their way down the mountainside toward the cover of trees and overhanging ledges. It was slow going, and Greg grit his teeth as his arm began to throb with pain. Thunder rumbled around them and an occasional crack of lightning spurred them to move faster and find cover.

At last they reached a lower plateau, crossing a narrow band of hard snow and climbing up to a small, relatively flat patch of grass. In the face of the rock was a cave that had been hollowed back into the side of the cliff, lying just under a protective promontory. To the right was a small spring where a thin stream of water oozed from cracks in the rock and trickled downhill.

"In here," she said, just as the rain began to fall and pummel the ground around them. They dashed under the cover of the ledge and brushed aside the tangle of bushes that covered the mouth of the cave.

Once inside, Anne shivered from the cold and the trauma and Greg sat on the hard ground, dazed by the pain that had numbed his arm and his brain.

She moved over and knelt down in front of him, a grave expression on her face.

"It's only a flesh wound, Anne. Don't look so worried."

"But you've lost quite a bit of blood."

"Not much," he slurred, still dazed by the ache that was punctuated now and then by a sharp stabbing pain. "I'm fine, really I am."

"Stop trying to be so macho, Greg. This isn't the O.K. Corral and you're certainly not John Wayne."

"Are you sure?" he said, smiling a bit as he looked over at her. "Okay, then, Nurse Jane, what do you suggest?"

Frustration leaped across her face. "I don't know anything about bullet wounds, but...well, I know we have to clean the area first. Is the bullet still in there?"

"No, Anne." Greg sighed almost impatiently. "I told you, it's only a flesh wound."

She reached for her pack and pulled out the canteen. She ripped his sleeve down the rest of the way and wadded it up, then saturated it with the water. "I'll wash it first with this, but then I want to build a fire so I'll have some hot water to clean it better."

He glanced down at his torn shirt. "You know how much that cost me at Eddie Bauer's?"

She looked up and smirked. "Ask me if I care."

"You're a hard woman, Anne Holdenfield. A hard woman."

He tried to sit still and not wince as she carefully washed the jagged wound in his arm. The flesh was torn, but once the dried blood was removed they could tell the bullet had grazed him without penetration. No muscle or bone was torn.

"I think you're going to live," she declared.

"Don't sound so disappointed about it."

"I'm not disappointed, I'm worried. It's not a deep wound, but it's bad enough, and we need to get you some antibiotics."

"Call up the local pharmacy," he said, leaning back against the wall of the cave and closing his eyes. "I'm sure they'll deliver."

Anne sat quietly thinking for a moment. "We're going to get you over to the ranger station. It's only a half day's hike from here...maybe three-quarters in your condition."

He opened his eyes and scowled at her. "I'm not going to any ranger station. I told you I'm fine."

"You are not fine, and Jack Bennett always has a supply of antibiotics on hand. He'll be able to fix you up."

"I don't want to be fixed up," he snapped.

"Tough," she replied.

With his good arm, he reached for her elbow and made her face him. "Look, Anne, I don't know what happened this afternoon, but I intend to find out. We were shot at and I want to know why."

She sighed. "Okay, we'll tell Jack about it and he can check it out."

Greg's face hardened like the cold rock walls around him. "We will not tell Jack Bennett a damn thing. We will not tell anyone a damn thing. Is that understood?"

Anne's chin shot out. "Don't play the imperious warrior with me, Greg Fisher. And let go of my elbow; it's about to break." He loosened his grip and she sat back against the wall, hugging her knees. "We have to tell someone about this. Some maniac is up on this mountain taking potshots at people. And that is a definite no-no."

Greg leaned forward and rested his elbow on his bent thigh. "Listen to me for a minute, Anne. You saw the equipment that was up there. That was no eighteenth-century mine...or if it was, then it's been reopened. There were new ore carts, new picks and freshly dug holes. Someone is up there mining that place."

"Jack Bennett could tell us if there are any operating mines in this area and who holds the claims on them."

"Have you got something going with this Jack Bennett jerk?"

She looked annoyed but said nothing.

"I take that as no," Greg said. "So can we forget about him for a minute? Now look, suppose—just suppose—that this was really old Pervis's mine. And suppose that somebody like me has been looking for it. But he finds it first and realizes that there is still gold in them thar hills."

Despite the attempt at a joke, Anne noticed him wince from a sharp stab of pain in his arm. "I'm going to light a fire, Greg. We've got to clean that with warm water."

"It can wait."

She stood up and overruled him. "No, it can't." She went out into the rain and in a few minutes was back dripping wet with some logs and a small tinder bundle of cliff-rose bark and squaw wood from the trees. She gathered some rocks from the entrance of the cave and laid them in a semicircle around the wall.

She laid the logs, then, using the matches from her pack, lit the tender, blowing it until the flame caught and held. Within minutes they had a fire, and the rock wall behind them acted as a reflector, drawing the smoke upward and forcing the heat back over them.

She put on a pan of water to heat and then sat down by Greg. His eyes were closed and she pressed her hand against his forehead to see if he had a fever. He opened his eyes and looked at her.

"I'm fine. Now are you quite finished with all this domestic stuff? You shouldn't have gone to so much trouble with the fire. We're not going to be here that long."

She nodded emphatically. "You're darn right we're not. Tomorrow morning we're leaving early for the ranger station."

"Oh, no, we're not."

"Oh, yes, we are."

Greg sat forward and glared at her. "Listen to me, you hardheaded broad—"

"Sticks and stones don't faze me, Fisher. But if you ever call me a broad again, I'll knock your big fat block off."

He sat back, surprised at her indignation, and humbled somewhat by her right to be angry. "Sorry," he murmured. "But dammit, I want you to listen to me."

"I'm listening, I'm listening."

"Good, because I'm going to tell you how it is. I didn't come all the way to Colorado, climb for days on end across these god-awful rocks, ford icy streams, get shot at and put up with your endless disdain of me just to go tell some ranger what I've found. I came here to find the Hole-in-the-Sky Mine. I came here to win ten thousand dollars. I came here to find something to write about for the next five years and assure my status at the university.'' His face moved closer to hers. ''And that, my lovely lady. . .now, was that better than hardheaded broad?''

She nodded without a smile.

''And that, my lovely lady, is exactly what I intend to do. Now we will forget about this Jeff Bennett heartthrob of yours—''

''Jack, not Jeff.''

''Whatever. We're going to forget about him and we, or I—if you don't want to go—are going to head back up to that mine and find out what in hell is going on.''

Anne used her jacket to remove the hot pan from the fire and set it on a flat rock. She dropped the ripped sleeve into the pan and then with a stick fished it back out. Holding it in the air to cool it enough to handle, she regarded Greg closely. ''And you have the nerve to call me stubborn,'' she said. ''You're a damn fool, Greg Fisher. You don't know what's going on up there and you could get yourself killed.''

''Listen, if I don't win this bet, I'm going to suffer a fate worse than death anyway. I told you what those guys expect of me if I lose. If the university found out that I had selected three students for the Vanguard program on the basis of a lost bet, they'd rip the rug out from under me so fast I wouldn't know what hit.'' His face grew pensive and serious. ''I have to win this bet, Anne. Regardless of my stupidity in making it in the first place, I have to win it."

"Are you willing to compromise?" she asked.

"With whom?"

"With me."

"Over what?"

She touched the rag and found it cool enough to handle, so she picked it off the stick and laid it against his arm. He closed his eyes and grimaced as the heat penetrated the open wound.

"Over what?" he asked again, this time through clenched teeth, his eyes still closed.

She tried to be careful as she washed it, not wanting to cause him any more pain than he already felt. "If you'll go with me to the ranger station—now wait until I finish, Greg."

He had opened his eyes halfway and was scowling at her, but he let her finish.

"Just to get some antibiotics," she continued. "Just to let Jack take a look at your arm and see what he can do, then we can go back up to the mine. I'll go with you."

"And what are we supposed to tell old Jack when he asks how I got a hole in my arm?"

"We'll figure something out. We have all night and tomorrow to think about it. We won't tell him what really happened if you don't want to."

He was watching her closely, his gaze narrowed on her face.

"Don't look at me like that," she snapped. "I give you my word I won't tell a soul. But I'm telling you right here and now that if you don't go get that arm checked, I will not go with you to the mine and I'll shout out what happened from the highest peak around here to anyone who will listen."

"Some compromise," he muttered. "Back where I come from we call that blackmail."

"Call it what you will, Greg. Those are my terms."

He studied her for a long moment. "What is it about you, Anne Holdenfield, that makes me like you even when you're playing Ivan the Terrible?"

She smiled sweetly. "My charm?"

"Hardly," he said with a grumble, looking down at his arm as she pulled the cloth away. The jagged tear in his skin looked better now that it was clean, but it was throbbing with a dull, continuous ache.

"Now," she said, all brisk and businesslike, pulling a nylon camisole from her pack. "I'm going to wrap this around it so no dirt can get in, and this should keep it until we get to—"

"I know, I know," he interrupted. "I don't want to hear that joker's name again."

"I believe you're jealous." She smiled.

"You must be joking. Me, jealous?"

He watched her turn away to put the supplies back in her pack and he leaned his head against the wall. *Yes, you jealous, Fisher. Not a very familiar emotion, is it?* But then none of the emotions he had felt with Anne were familiar. He had definitely crossed into new territory with her and he wasn't sure whether to keep exploring it or head back for safer, surer ground. For there was one thing about Anne Holdenfield—she scared the hell out of him.

"Don't you want something to eat?"

He closed his eyes with a smile. "I want a pizza."

"Sorry. How about freeze-dried ham with noodles?"

"I just lost my appetite. Come on," he said, holding his right hand out to her. "Get off your knees for a while and sit with me."

She set down the pot she was going to cook in and came over beside him. His right arm draped around her back and his hand rested on the side of her hip. Her head dropped to his shoulder. They sat like that for a while, watching the fire and listening to the pounding rain outside the cave.

"Just think," Greg mused. "If Willard Hopkins hadn't backed out on me, I'd be sitting here with him right now."

"Hopefully not this close," she said.

He slid down the wall and lay on his back, pulling her on top of him. "Hopefully not this close, either," he said, a grin spreading across his face.

"What are you doing, Greg?" she asked, trying to sound perturbed but not succeeding very well.

"What do you think I'm doing?"

"What about your arm?"

"Oh, it'll be mad because it missed out on all the fun, I'm sure, but that's the breaks."

She shook her head and smiled down at him. "You really are a pill, do you know that?"

His eyes were serious and warm as he looked up at her and ran his fingers through her hair. "Yeah," he whispered low, "you're special, too, Anne." He pulled her head down, forcing her mouth to meet his. She was warm and soft and moist and she healed him with her hands and her lips, making him forget the pain in his arm, and the mine above them, and the ten thousand dollars, and the rain, and the fire, and...

Chapter Eleven

The sun was just peeking over the rise of mountains when they packed up and left the cave for their hike to the ranger station. During the night Greg's arm had given him a lot of trouble, so he had slept very little. He polished off his flask of bourbon and that helped to dull the pain somewhat. Maybe Anne was right, maybe some pain pills and an antibiotic would help. But there was no way he was going to admit that she was right about it. He was going to do nothing to shift the balance of power too far in her favor.

The rain had stopped in the early evening and left the mountainside with a clean, fresh smell. Lines from Robert Browning's poem—"The year's at the spring and day's at the morn"—came to mind, but he would have felt stupid telling Anne that, so he quoted them to himself as they left the cave and headed due east across a montane of moist upland slopes and dense, cool thickets of evergreens.

The trek took about five hours, with a forty-five-minute stop for lunch. Greg was realistic enough to know that if Anne had been by herself—without him

tagging along, stopping every few minutes to rest—
she could have made it in half that time.

Anne, however, wasn't thinking about time. She
was thinking about how pale he looked and how he
kept grimacing as the pain repeatedly jabbed at his
arm. She wanted to lighten his pack to help him, but
he insisted that he was fine and she knew better than
to press him too hard or he was liable to fly off the
handle at her again. It didn't look as if it would take
too much for that to happen today.

Instead of lightening his load, she tried to take his
mind off the pain by talking, and if he noticed her
unusual chattering, he didn't say anything about it.
They went over and over what they had seen at the
mining site, trying to piece together the historic facts
with the present reality.

"It's those graves that really bother me the most,"
he said. "Who were they? If there were Chinese who
worked with Pervis Johnson, did he bury them and
write those epitaphs in Chinese? And what was that
other grave with the strange markings, the one that
was separated from the others? Who's buried there?"

There were more questions than answers at this
point, but Greg was determined to find those answers. It had become a much more intriguing adventure than just finding a long-lost mine.

"I should be getting tenured at the university next
year; this discovery and the subsequent brilliant articles that I will write should cinch it."

Anne rolled her eyes. "And I suppose you'll claim
that you found it singlehandedly."

"No, no," he said. "I'll give credit where credit is due."

She narrowed her eyes at him. "How come I don't like the sound of that?"

His answer was a wickedly mysterious grin.

They arrived at the ranger station in the early afternoon and were met by Jack Bennett, who was just coming in from gathering wood.

"Howdy, Anne. Didn't expect to see you until mail day."

"Hi, Jack. I want you to meet a friend of mine, Greg Fisher. He's up here for a couple of weeks on a Princeton study of bighorn, and we've been working together on it."

Greg shook hands with the ranger and tried to ignore Anne's grin, which he saw out of the corner of his eye. So this was the guy he had been jealous of all night? Jack Bennett was at least fifty-five, bald, and stood about five feet three inches in boots.

"What happened to you?" he asked, frowning at the rag wrapped around Greg's arm.

"That's why we're here, Jack," Anne explained. "He had a bad fall up in Storm Pass and he tore it on a rock."

"Thought maybe you might have something to fix me up," Greg added.

"Well, I probably do. Come on inside and let's take a look at that."

They followed Jack into the station and Anne sidled up to Greg, whispering, "Still jealous?"

He looked down his nose at her. "I never was."

She smirked "Sure you weren't."

Once they were inside, Jack told them to sit around the table and he poured them all a cup of coffee. Then he pulled a chair over, straddled it backward and began to peel away the crude but effective wrapping that Anne had put on Greg's arm.

"Whoo! That's a nasty hole. You got that from a rock?"

"I don't know," Greg lied easily. "All I know is I was falling and when I stopped and looked down at my arm, I had this."

"Did you clean it?" he asked Anne.

"Yes, but I didn't have any medicine other than some first-aid cream."

Jack stood up and put on a kettle of water to boil. "Well, I'll clean it again and put salve on it. You allergic to anything?"

"Not that I know of," Greg said.

"Okay, then let me go find the medicine while that water heats." When he left the room, Anne and Greg just looked at each other, but avoided saying much lest they give any of the lies away.

"Real coffee," Greg said with a sigh after taking a long, hot sip. "Tastes great."

"What's wrong with my coffee?" she asked, frowning.

"Nothing if you don't mind it tasting like it's been dredged up by some offshore oil tanker."

"That's it," she snapped. "From now on, you can make your own."

"Good idea," he said, then smiled at her. "Best suggestion you've had all day."

Jack came back into the room before Anne could retaliate, but she wasn't about to forget this. She'd get him later.

Jack pulled the kettle off the burner of the old iron stove and dipped a clean cloth into it. He didn't seem to mind the heat on his hands as he carried it over to the table and wrapped the steaming rag around Greg's arm. He might not have minded, but Greg sure as hell did—he almost came out of the chair when the hot cloth first touched his gaping flesh.

"Need a bullet to bite on?" Jack asked when he saw the look on Greg's face.

The wet cloth was pulled away and Greg took a deep breath and let it out slowly. He glanced over at Anne and smiled when he saw the worried expression on her face. "I'm going to live," he reassured her. "You're stuck with me a little longer."

If Jack noticed anything more than a professional relationship between Anne and Greg, he made no comment about it. He went about his own business of doctoring the wound with an antiseptic and then handing Greg some antibiotic salve. "That should fix you up now." He looked over at Anne. "Where are you heading from here?"

She unconsciously glanced at Greg, then looked back at Jack. "We're going up toward the Castles. There's a herd up there that I've been keeping an eye on. I'd like for Greg to see them."

"Well, why don't you spend the night here and start out in the morning? I've got that old bunkhouse out back and the mattresses aren't too shabby."

Anne stole another glance at Greg and noticed the weariness in his eyes. Even if he wanted to take off for the mine now, they wouldn't make it far. He had gone about as far as he could go today. "Yes, we'll stay," she said, taking the matter in her own hands, and she was positive she saw a sign of relief in Greg's drooped shoulders.

They had dinner that night with Jack, and he fixed them a venison stew and hot biscuits. He had learned how to cook well on the wood stove, and Greg was positive it was the best meal he had ever had. He went back time and time again for another bowl of stew and ate at least half a dozen biscuits himself.

"That arm sure hasn't affected his appetite, has it?" Jack said with a laugh.

"He's right-handed," Anne said. "He can still reach for whatever he wants." She blushed when she caught Greg's eye and realized how appropriately that comment described his behavior the previous night in the cave.

After dinner they went out to the bunkhouse, claiming they were tired and wanted to get an early start. This was all true, but they politely omitted the fact that they couldn't wait to be in each other's arms again—fatigue or no fatigue.

The bunkhouse was very small but, as Jack had said, the bed wasn't too shabby.

"It's a bed, anyway" was the way Greg put it, pulling her down on top of him. "And that's all that matters."

She smiled, straddling him on the lumpy mattress. "Compared to the hard ground we've been sleeping on, this feels like a waterbed."

Greg's hands cupped her hips and pulled them down more tightly against his. "Moves real nicely with us, doesn't it?" he said, guiding her body into motion with his.

"I see what you mean," she whispered faintly, closing her eyes as the rhythm took over her mind. She leaned over him and he pulled the band from her hair, letting it fall across her shoulders and into his face. He grabbed a handful of it and gripped it tight, while his other hand kept a firm hold on her hip. Her mouth dropped down over his, opening and closing, her tongue following the curve of his lips, meeting the tip of his tongue, then letting the draw of his mouth pull her farther down, her breasts flattened against his chest, her legs still straddling his hips.

She bit at his lower lip and drew her tongue lightly down his chin and neck. Raising up, she began to open the buttons of his shirt, then peeled it back and let her hands run across the rough skin of his chest.

The hand that had been grasping her hip so tightly fell to the bed and she knew that his arm was hurting him badly. So, on this night, she was the aggressor, the conqueror, the reaper of the spoils. He lay beneath her and she showered his body with all the exquisite torture that he had inflicted on her time and time again. And his low moans filled her with a reckless power that spurred her on to a feverish pitch of sexuality that she had never known or experienced before.

And afterward they lay against each other, their bodies damp and warm and totally exhausted.

As she lay in the crook of Greg's right arm, his fingers stroked her temple, winding through the wet tendrils that hung over her forehead.

"Does your arm hurt badly?" she asked.

"Not too much," he said. "The salve helped a bit."

"Will you be able to sleep all right?"

"I think so." He smiled to himself. "I was just lying here thinking."

"About what?"

"About you." His fingers wound through her hair and pulled it back from her face. "I was trying to imagine what you must have been like as a little girl."

"I was a tomboy all the way," she said, smiling.

"I figured as much. You didn't play with dolls and dishes and all that stuff?"

"Some," she admitted. "But most of the time I was out collecting bugs. I had the best grasshopper collection on Adams Street."

He chuckled softly. "I wish I had known you then. I wish we had lived next door to each other."

She turned her head and kissed his chest. "But you would have moved away when your father was transferred to another base. You would have left me."

Silence pervaded the air around them as the impact of what she had said sunk in to both of them. He would have left her then and, as would happen in a couple of days, he would leave her now.

She could not bear to think about it, so she tried to block it from her mind. And the emotional and physical fatigue from the day finally wrapped around them and carried them away together in the night.

After a hearty breakfast with Jack, they thanked him for all his help and were on their way by eight o'clock. Once out of sight and earshot of the ranger station, Anne stopped and turned to Greg.

"Are you sure you want to do this?" she asked.

"Listen, Anne, I'm not going back to Princeton with my tail between my legs."

She smiled. "No, I can't imagine you ever doing that."

He reached out to cup her face with his hand. "If you don't want to go, you don't have to. I'll understand completely. I've taken up enough of your time as it is."

She stared at him for a moment, and a hardness appeared in her eyes. "You've taken a hell of a lot more than that, Greg Fisher." But before he could react, she turned away and resumed walking. "And if you think I'm going to let you go by yourself and take all the glory in this, you're crazier than I thought."

He tried to process what she had said, but he really wasn't sure what she meant by taking more than just her time. If he had been truthful with himself, he would have admitted that he wasn't sure he wanted to know. That might entail an emotional commitment that he wasn't certain he could make right now. So without further comment, he followed her up the side of the mountain, focusing his thoughts on the mine and the reason he was there in the first place. Focusing on anything but Anne Holdenfield and what she might represent in his life.

Chapter Twelve

It was a hard full day's hike back up to the rocks that hid the mine and the secret passageway to it. They decided to camp for the night on the plateau just below it and then go up there early the next morning. Here on the green bench there were a few gnarled trees and some rocky overhangs to give protection from the cold night wind.

Greg was up first the next morning, packing up his gear so they could get going. Anne slowly opened her eyes and stared at him. "This has got to be a first," she said sleepily.

"I don't want to waste any more time," he said as he rolled up his sleeping bag and attached it to the base of his pack. "There was a time limit on this bet, remember?"

"How could I forget?" she grumbled. "That's all you've talked about for the last two days."

"Well, it's pretty important."

"So I've surmised. Okay, Fisher," she said, sighing. "I'm getting up. You can stop pacing back and forth now. Do I get breakfast?"

"Here," he said, handing her a plate of burnt toast and a cup of coffee.

Within minutes they had left the campsite and were climbing over the craggy rocks and abrupt ridges that defined this high barren landscape. This part of the trip was the most difficult for Greg because it normally took two hands to pull himself up over the rocks and to help him keep his balance. Even though his arm was much better now, he was still favoring it and he tried to be very careful not to slip and injure it more.

They bent down low and moved quietly across the rimrock overlooking the canyon below. They didn't want to take any chances of being spotted. They had come too far to be driven off again. This time they were going to get some answers. The short vegetation helped to conceal them as they made their way to the narrow opening in the rocks that would lead them to the mine.

At the opening Greg stopped and held Anne's hand. "Are you sure you want to go? You can wait here if you want. I'll understand."

She stood on tiptoe and kissed him lightly. "You're not going to get rid of me that easy, Fisher."

He reached around her with his arm and pulled her up tight against him. The blue of his eyes had turned dark and serious and his mouth was drawn as he looked down into her face. "I...I don't think I'm going to find it very easy saying good-bye to you."

Her breath quickened and her heart began to pound in her chest. "I don't want to talk about it." She didn't even want to think about it.

"We need to."

She sighed heavily. "Easy or not, Greg, saying good-bye is exactly what we will be doing in a few days." *Saying good-bye forever.*

His eyes swept across her face and his mouth came down on hers, hard and demanding, while his hand held the back of her head so she could not escape. When he finally released her mouth, he spoke low against her cheek. "We have to talk, Anne. As soon as we find out what's going on here and head back to the trailer, we have to talk."

"Yes," she said, wondering what they could possibly say to each other that would change anything. The end result would be the same. They would say good-bye and go their own ways, he back to Princeton and his students, she to begin the long, painful process of mending her heart and soul again.

She eased out of his arms and turned toward the opening in the rocks. He followed silently as she pushed and plunged her way through the thick shrubs, disappearing once again in that hole in the sky.

They took their time going through the passageway, hoping not to loosen any rocks that might tumble and announce their arrival. This was intended to be a surprise attack.

When they reached the far side, they crouched down low against the boulders. Anne pulled out her scope from her pack and handed the binoculars to Greg.

"You look from the center of this opening to the left," Greg whispered. "I'll cover the area to the right."

The whole area before them was eerie in its setting and content. An odd assortment of old and new created the image of a place that had just barely survived a bomb attack. Buildings crumbled and weeds grew around them but, as the new ore carts and cable attested, life went on.

After a few minutes they heard a noise, and both of them trained their binoculars in the same direction. It was the sound of metal wheels along a metal track and it was coming from the new gravel deposits sliding down the side of the mountain. The noise grew louder and soon they saw a man emerge, hat down low on his head, a heavy metal chain tied around his waist and gripped tightly in his hands as he pulled the cart along the track an inch at a time.

They watched, fascinated, as he stopped, then shoveled up the deposits from the cart and dumped them into a thirty-foot sluice box made from whipsawed lumber, where jets of water from the melting snow transported the loosened materials down the slope and where riffles of stone on the bottom of the sluice caught any particles of gold in the channels between the rocks. A burro and several large burlap sacks waited patiently at the bottom of the slope.

They continued to watch the little man as he worked with almost feverish intensity, dumping the ore deposits into the water.

"How old is that guy?" Greg whispered.

"Must be eighty at least," Anne said. "I think he's Oriental."

Greg lowered his glasses and sat still while he thought. "We've got to get over to him without him seeing us."

Anne looked around the small valley. "I think if we go along that ridge we can stay behind cover until we're just above him. If he goes down to the bottom of the sluice box to count his winnings or if he goes back to that pile of deposits, then we can sneak up on him."

"Let's give it a try, then," Greg said.

They stuffed the binoculars and scope back into Anne's pack and carefully moved out of the crevasse and around the rocks, staying low behind the cover of vegetation and gnarled pine. It was slow going, but they moved at a fairly steady rate around the rim until they reached a spot about twenty-five yards above the old man. From here, they got a better look at him in his faded dungarees and worn felt hat, working without rest on a mine that had probably played out over seventy-five years ago.

"Is that his rifle down there?" Anne asked, pointing to a spot next to the burro.

"I think so. Here's what we're going to do. You go back down that way and try to get to the gun."

"The burro will probably make noise."

"Then you'll have to move fast," he said. "I'll go around over here and try to reach him at the same time you get to the rifle."

She sighed. "Why am I doing this, Fisher? I must be out of my mind."

He chuckled and gave her a quick kiss on the forehead. "Once you have the rifle you can shoot me and put me out of your misery."

"Don't tempt me," she mumbled, adding, "Well, here goes nothing." She turned and sidled along the ledge, keeping close to the ground behind the bushes and weeds. He watched her go and then started in the opposite direction toward the old guy. Greg kept looking back at Anne, trying to judge her distance from the gun so that he could reach the prospector at the same time.

When he was just above him, Greg jumped down and grabbed the startled old man from behind. He wrapped his right arm around the small frail body and held him tight while Anne scrambled for the rifle near the feet of the bucking, braying mule.

She grabbed it and climbed up the slope, holding it out in front of her as she pointed it at the old miner.

"Please," he cried, almost pitifully. "For please!"

"We didn't come here to cause you any harm, old man," Greg said as he held him tight. "So don't do anything to make us hurt you, okay?"

The man nodded. "Okay."

"I'm going to let you loose now, all right?"

He nodded once more and Greg let go of the old man's body. A split second later, the man bent down with a speed and agility that defied his age, spun around and had a pick in his hand, which he was holding high above his head like a knight with a sword.

Greg sighed. "Dammit, man! Don't you know we could shoot you?"

"Go ahead," he said in a heavily accented voice.

"You don't want to die."

"I die all my life. And I defend this mine all my life, too. I die defending it."

"We're not here to take your mine," Anne said, feeling at once sorry for the poor man.

He looked from Greg to Anne and back to Greg again. "Then why you here?"

"You shot me," Greg growled. "Two days ago, you pointed that rifle at us and shot me."

The man shrugged. "You still alive."

"By pure accident," Greg snapped. "Now I'm here to find out why you did it and what you are doing here, and then we'll be on our way and you can go back to hacking away at this mountain."

The man raised himself up to a full five feet. "This my mountain. I earned it and I defend it against all marauders."

"We're not marauders," Greg huffed impatiently. "We are here on a scientific study."

"What kind of study you do?"

"I'm looking for a place called the Hole-in-the-Sky Mine."

The man did not lower his pick. "I not know it."

"It was worked by a man named Pervis Johnson."

The pick seemed to quiver in the air above the man's head. "Why you want to find it?"

"Do you know the mine? Is this it?"

"I ask you question first," he insisted.

"I'm looking for it because no one has ever found it and many people doubt it even existed."

"So why you think different?"

Greg paused for a moment as he regarded the man's stiff, proud posture despite the long years of back-breaking work. His gaze swung around the old mining camp, cataloging in his mind everything that was there. Finally he looked back at the old man. "Because this is Pervis Johnson's mine." Their eyes caught and held. "Isn't it?"

The pick slowly lowered to his side and then, with a flick of his wrist, he flipped it to the ground, where it stuck in the loose dirt. He removed his hat, revealing a short crop of white hair, and he wiped his forehead with the back of his arm.

"I know someday it will be over. I tell myself this. I know it to be true." He shrugged philosophically. "So, it is over."

"What's over?" Anne asked, lowering the gun to her side. This man posed no threat, and she wasn't about to continue intimidating him with his own rifle. Still, from the quick look she received from Greg, she knew she'd better hang on to it for a while longer.

The old man looked longingly at the ore deposits that lay all around him. He stared at the sluice that carried it downstream. He glanced at the empty sacks that lay at the mule's feet. "The vein is at end of my pick. I know this. I smell it."

"Pervis Johnson said the same thing," Greg pointed out.

The old man spat onto the ground. "I not hear that name for many years, but still too soon."

"What do you know about Johnson?"

"I know too much."

"Will you tell us?" Anne asked, stepping closer to the two men.

He sighed and slipped his hat back on. "Come," he said, leading the way down the pile of loose gravel to a small log hut set amidst the rubble of a previous century. He opened the heavy wooden door that was hinged with straps of leather and invited them inside.

It was one room, spartan and clean to the point of immaculate. When he noticed Anne's amazement, he said, "I know my father's friends and my father's father's friends die from disease. It very unclean then. Here. Sit."

They sat down on the hard cot, and the old man sat cross-legged on the floor nearby. "You want to know about Johnson," he stated lethargically.

"Yes."

"My father bury him."

"Pervis died here?"

The old eyes lifted up to Greg. "My father's father kill him."

"Killed Johnson?" he asked. "Why?"

The man spat on the floor, then bent over and wiped the spot with his sleeve. "Why, you say. Because Pervis Johnson an animal. He kill many men, he kill women, too."

"Killed them how?"

"My father's father and his friends, they work up here for Johnson. He give them little food, none of it good, not good shelter. He make them work many hours, work them hard, beat them, too. He take the wives and make them his own. Many women who live here die from cold and no good food and much disease. Johnson, he not care. He want more gold. More, more, always more. Many people suffer under Pervis Johnson.''

''But he apparently went to town quite often,'' Greg said. ''Why didn't everyone leave while he was gone?''

The old man nodded slowly. ''One man—he was friend of my father's father. But he turn bad. He was Johnson's best man. Watch over others when Johnson not here. Watches and beats and tells bad lies about the men.''

''So your grandfather killed Johnson.''

The old man stared hard at Greg, daring him not to understand. ''Johnson kill the wife of my father's father. He kill my father's sister. What else was there to do?''

''Is Johnson the one who is buried in that grave with the strange markings?''

The man nodded.

''What does the marker say?''

''It is ancient curse.'' The old man sat perfectly still, his voice a slow, even monotone. '''No rest will come to Pervis Johnson.' ''

Anne rubbed her hands on the tops of her thighs, feeling goose bumps rise along her skin. ''How old was your father when...when all of this happened?''

''Young. I do not know how old.''

''What happened after Johnson was killed?'' Greg wanted to know.

''The men work here to mine the gold for many years. Some become rich. Some die. My father mine until I am ten and then we go to town. I go to school, but I come back when I am eighteen." He looked toward the open doorway that framed the stream and the mountainside where his dreams and his life lay. "This is where I stay."

"But you've never become rich," Anne said. "Why do you stay?"

"It not matter. This is where I belong."

"Don't you think the gold might be all played out?" Greg asked.

The man slowly shook his head. "It there," he insisted. "It lay waiting, but it there."

THE SUN WAS HANGING in the western sky before Anne and Greg were ready to leave. They had had lunch with the old man, whose name they learned was Lin Chung, and then they had toured the whole mining area and Greg had taken several rolls of film. After he had all the proof he needed of the mine's existence, he and Anne decided they had better go. The three of them walked in the direction of the exit in the cliff, and the old man was stoically quiet and subdued.

"I'm not wanting to ruin this for you, Lin," Greg insisted. "But this is what I came to find."

The old man nodded philosophically. "I have no mining claim. When others know, they will come and take all this away from me. Then I know it is time to die." Without another word, Lin Chung turned and walked back toward his deposits and his wooden sluice box and his mule.

Greg and Anne watched him go; then, in humbled silence, they began their laborious climb toward the crevasse in the rocks.

Greg stopped and turned around, staring back at Lin. He had reached his ore bucket and was shoveling it once again into the water-filled sluice. He looked back at Anne. "Wait here. I'll be right back."

She sat down on a large boulder and watched as Greg climbed back down the rocks, still favoring his left arm as he moved carefully in the direction of Lin Chung. She saw him walk up to the man and stop. There they stood and talked for several minutes. And to her surprise, she saw Greg stick out his hand and Lin met him halfway with his own.

After several more minutes he climbed back up the steep slope and rejoined her. "What was that all about?" she asked.

But he only shook his head. "Just something I forgot to ask him," he answered cryptically. And whether she was being melodramatic or not, she felt a huge rift open between them. The beginning of the end was at hand. Although it was a minor point, to be sure, he was already excluding her from his find. It was a way of breaking off the tie that had bound them so closely the past few days. It was a way of getting back some of his lost independence. It saddened her and yet she understood it. In a way, she was even glad of it, because it would make it that much less difficult for her to break her own ties to him.

After puzzling over the map for a long time, Anne decided to take another route home. They would be going across a different ridge, and it would cut at least a day and a half off their travel time.

The whole journey home was much as she had expected it to be. They talked and laughed and joked but avoided at all costs the topic that was foremost on both their minds. Greg was positively jovial over finding the mine, and that helped to ease the tension between them.

"Do you believe it, Anne? We're the first, the first ever to find that place. Lin Chung has been carrying on up there for years and years and no one knew anything about it. That, to me, is incredible. How could no one know?"

"This is wild country, Greg. There are still many places left to explore. And very few people ever make it up that high. It's just too difficult."

He chuckled. "Oh, Lin Chung sure was a character, wasn't he?"

"I feel sorry for him," she said, biting her tongue the minute the words slipped out. Who was she to say that Greg shouldn't tell the world what he had found? He had found it fair and square, and she had no right to pass judgment on that.

Greg just looked at her and said nothing.

They camped that night by a stream and ate fruit and ham and candy bars. The sky above them was a velvet tapestry of twinkling lights as they sat around their campfire after dinner.

But it was the second night before Greg approached what they had been avoiding for two days. "Remember how I said we have to talk?"

Anne stared straight ahead at the fire and hugged her knees with her arms. "I remember."

"This is difficult for me, Anne, because...well, because I've never known anyone like you before. I've been kind of...oh, I guess you'd call it footloose and fancy free. I've never made any attachments, never had a desire to form any. I just approached everything as one big game." He picked up a stick and poked the fire with it. "I don't know, maybe that was all wrong. Maybe I should have taken life more seriously, planned things a little more carefully. Instead, I've just rolled along from one day to the next, unmindful of anything more than having a good time." He looked over at her. "Do you know what I'm saying?"

She stared back at him and nodded. "Yes, I do, Greg."

"What I'm trying to say in all of this is that you're the first person I've ever known that I wanted to form some sort of attachment with. I've never cared about being with a woman more than once or twice...before you."

She tried to laugh. "You were stuck with me. That's the only difference."

"No, it's not. Everything about you is different. You've changed my whole outlook on male-female relationships." He chuckled low. "In fact, lady, you rewrote the entire book on them."

She smiled over at him but didn't say anything. What was there to say at this point? The denouement was already written. The actors were in place. All that was left was the call for action.

"I didn't know what it meant to have an intimate relationship with a woman and be her friend, too. With me it's always been one or the other." He shrugged sheepishly. "And I have to admit, it was more often the former. I don't know exactly how you...how you feel about me. I'm not even clear about my own feelings right now. But I do know that I don't want to leave you." He looked up at her, and as hard as she tried, she couldn't look away. His blue eyes held her riveted and she could not escape. "I want to work something out where we can be together, Anne."

She sat very still, afraid to speak for fear she would begin to cry. Why did things have to get this complicated? Why had she let it go so far?

She took a deep breath and plunged in. "I haven't been very successful in love, Greg. Even my marriage fell apart...no, I take that back. There was nothing to fall apart. It never congealed in the first place. I thought—until you came along—that I knew what I wanted in life. I thought I knew what kind of man I was attracted to. But you changed all that for me, too."

She sighed and looked over at the fire, seeing the future rise before her in the leaping blue flames. "I do know that I don't want to give up my career. I've worked very hard for it, and it has held me together when nothing else seemed to. There have been times when I thought I was falling apart." She waved her hand around her. "All of this was the glue that kept me whole. I've set my life out before me, Greg. I've got it all mapped out. And you're settled in yours. I'm not sure that we should mess with that. I think we have to be realistic and practical. We met, we cared for each other, we found each other mutually...attractive. But my life is here in Colorado and yours is in New Jersey. I have no intention of living there and playing the social scene with you or anyone else. I don't mean that to sound cold or like some sort of militant feminist. It's just the way things are for me." She chuckled lightly. "And I can't quite imagine you spending the rest of your life traipsing through the mountains, either. You're a sociable person. You need other people around you, and I think that's wonderful...for you." She stopped and looked over at him for a long moment. "Please, Greg, please be realistic with me. Please don't make this any harder than it already is."

He sat in thoughtful silence before he spoke again. "How does one just walk away from something like this? I thought I had the answers for everything, but I don't have the answer for this."

"I don't have the answer, either, Greg. I guess you just have to try to accept things the way they are and go on with your life. Once we get back into our own routines I'm sure it will be easier." *Lies and more lies.* She knew it would never become easier, but she tried to convince herself of that all the same.

He looked at her to see if the lie showed as plainly on her face as he was sure it did on his. Neither of them was going to find this easy, and inside they both knew it. But she looked away so he wouldn't see the truth in her eyes.

The sound of a wolf punctuated the night, and they both lifted their heads to listen to the woeful sound.

"How close is that?" Greg asked, trying not to let his apprehension show.

"I don't think we need to worry," she assured him. "He's several miles away. You should know by now how sound carries in these mountains."

He stood up and walked over to her and sat down beside her on the log. His arm came around her shoulder. "If he comes around, I'll save you from the big bad beast."

She elbowed him lightly in the stomach. "How reassuring."

He bent his head and kissed her neck, and he heard the soft sigh that fell from her lips. "This will only make it more difficult, Greg," she whispered.

"Convince me of that," he growled in a low, seductive breath against her skin. His mouth moved through her hair, exquisitely warm and persuasive, and her breath quickened in response to her body's longing. This man brought out colors in her that she never knew she had. Morning gold and coral, summer-sky blue, evening emerald, all velvet, all warm and soft. Where she had been gray and cold he had turned her to pastel and heat. And as his fingers worked loose the buttons of her shirt and his hand moved possessively to her breast, she knew she could deny him nothing. As much as she knew that this was the time to say no, to stop themselves before they caused the bond to weld even stronger, she knew she could not.

"I can't." She sighed, then turned to him and let the warmth of his hands heat her flesh. And she curved her palm around his face and to the back of his neck, urging his mouth down to meet hers in a passion that both knew could not last but was too good to deny.

Her hands trailed the length of him, loving the rough feel of his jeans as he pressed his body into hers. They lay back in the blue-green grass, and he spread open the front of her shirt. Leaning on one elbow, he let his other hand trail slowly over her breasts and stomach, watching the flesh rise from the chill of the night and the stroke of his fingers.

Her hand remained curved around his neck; the other lay limp against the ground. The wolf sounded again in the distance, but they paid it no heed this time, oblivious of the world that teemed with life all around them. Only their breath filled the night air, only their bodies reacted to the shift in the breeze, only their eyes saw passion reflected in the eyes of the other. Nothing else existed; nothing else mattered.

His fingers moved to the top of her jeans and the sound of the snap opening was magnified in the thin air. With a leisure that drove her to distraction, he slowly lowered the zipper and his hand snaked inside to follow the curve of her hip and thighs.

Don't ever leave me, she wanted to cry out, but the thrill of his fingers moving over her flesh tore all breath from her lungs. And it was only after an interminably torturous length of time that he helped her remove her jeans and then he removed his own clothes. And together they rode out the night, trying to forget that this would be the last such night for them, trying to push farther and farther away the inevitability of their good-byes.

THE BEAUTY OF THE DAY that surrounded them was awe-inspiring, the sounds of the birds a sweet trill, the fragrance of the wildflowers intoxicating. But in truth they saw and heard and smelled very little of it. They saw only their parting, heard only their good-byes, smelled only the bitter scent left when a flower petal has been crushed mercilessly underfoot.

After their night together they knew there was still much to say but no way to say it. Many times he started to tell her how much he cared. Many times she wanted to tell him that she had never felt before what she felt with him. But the words would never come. It was as if overnight a wall had been erected between them and nothing could penetrate it, no emotion would be allowed to escape or seep through the cracks.

It was not quite noon, and they were crossing one of the last major ridges before they would come to her trailer when Anne spotted something in the distance.

"Greg, get down!" she whispered.

He dropped down behind some vegetation beside her. "What is it?"

"I may be wrong, but I think it's Solomon." She pulled her scope from her pack and worked at getting a clear focus. She brushed a wisp of hair back and stared down the canyon at the meadow below. "Yes, I recognize the markings. It's him."

"What about Sheba?"

"I don't see...wait a minute...yes, there she is. But she's going up the cliff, away from him." She reached into her pack for the binoculars and handed them to him. "Here, take a look for yourself."

Greg lifted the glasses to his eyes and scanned the rocky knolls that were layered like steps down to the valley. At the base of the cliff he saw the sheep. "I think I see the ewe."

"She's over by the cliff to the left."

"Yes, that's the one, then."

"And Solomon is more to the center of the meadow, near that grouping of pine trees. See him?"

"Wait a minute...yes, I think...yes, there he is. That's the old boy, all right. Even I can recognize him. Wonder what Casanova has been up to all this time?"

Anne lowered the glasses and looked over at him with a grin. "You have to ask?"

"Hmm." He laughed. "Guess not. But where is Sheba going?"

Anne spun her scope in that direction. "I don't know, but she's halfway up the mountain. Maybe he'll follow in a few minutes."

But he didn't. They watched for twenty more minutes, and finally Solomon started to move. He looked off in the direction the ewe had gone and seemed almost to be watching her as she crossed over the ridge to the other side. Then he turned and walked in the opposite direction, heading into the thick forest of spruce and fir, away from the mate he had come so far to find.

Very slowly Anne lowered her scope to her lap. "Why are they splitting up?" she wondered aloud.

Greg stuffed the binoculars into her pack and stood up. "Why indeed?"

She watched him walk on ahead of her, and it was several seconds before she could move. Why indeed?

There was no rhyme or reason for Solomon and Sheba to have met in the first place. Therefore there was no reason for them to part. It was no different for Greg and her. What rhyme or reason could there have been for their meeting, falling in love and then parting? Certainly none that she could find.

The day seemed to drag interminably as the rift between them grew wider and wider. There was a light rain shower in the midafternoon, but it lasted only a short while and it left the grass wet and glistening. Thousands of tiny blue butterflies scattered at their feet and hovered around the warm rocks that nested in the meadows. A finch with red plumage flew out of the thick brush beside a stream and settled on the top of a nearby willow to watch Anne and Greg as they trudged through the marshy field. The hills were alive with the busy chatter of chipmunks in the trees and the quick scurry of martens darting between the fallen logs.

When they reached the clearing where Anne's trailer was, they stopped for a minute, neither of them willing to face the end of the journey. It looked small and somewhat forlorn nestled back in the trees, waiting for the woman who occupied it during the summer. It was a primitive type of living arrangement, but it had always suited her needs perfectly. Until now. Now the sight of it filled her with the most incredible loneliness she had ever known. Tomorrow she would remain behind while Greg made his way back down the mountain to town. Only she and her trailer and her sheep would remain.

The silence between them that evening was almost unbearable. But even worse was the light, inconsequential chatter that became the only conversation they could endure. They talked about the sheep; they talked about the mine. And though the subject lay like a dead weight between them, they never once talked about themselves.

Anne offered her cot to Greg for the night, but he opted instead for the hammock that hung outside the trailer. Neither spoke the words, but the implicit rules were evident to them both: This night they would sleep apart. And so shortly after dinner they both retired to their own beds, claiming a fatigue that had less to do with the physical trials of the past few days than with the emotional trial that had only just begun.

AS ALWAYS, THE SUN CAME UP. This day was no different from all the others—except in the small subtle ways of nature. New buds opened on trees, new flowers unfurled in the meadows, new butterflies were hatched into the air, a golden eagle flew for the first time, a squirrel left its mother and forayed out on its own. Each minute and each second brought something new and wondrous into the world.

To Anne it was another day like all the others, if you discounted the fact that the man she loved was kneeling on the ground in front of her, restuffing his pack to leave.

"Got enough candy bars left?" she said, smiling, trying for a lightness she didn't feel.

"Only two," he said, grinning up at her. "Think they'll last me until I get down to Ohio Creek Road?"

"Knowing you, I doubt it."

He went back to work on his pack, distributing the weight more evenly. He rerolled his sleeping bag and tied it to the bottom of the pack frame. Pulling out a pack of cigarettes, he shook one out in his hand and stuck it in his mouth. She noticed, though, that he didn't light it. It was all the little things she was noticing now. The way the light touched the top of his hair, the way his eyes avoided looking directly at her but, instead, shifted to the ground, to the trailer, to the sky, to the pack—barely grazing across her each time his gaze moved. She noticed him as he took the cigarette from his mouth, shifted it to the other hand, then slipped it back between his lips.

She watched his hands. Hands that had touched her and brought out wondrous things that she had not known existed in her. In a way, it would be easy to hate him for that. Before he came, she had been locked away inside herself, at least content with the way she was. Free from hurt and loneliness. But he had opened her up, let fly the pieces of her that she could no longer recapture and control. He had done that to her and now he was going to leave her.

"Well," he said, sticking the cigarette in his shirt pocket. "Guess I'd better be moseying along."

The humor of his statement didn't wash. It lay flat on the ground between them.

He cleared his throat. "You think I'll be able to hitch a ride to Gunnison once I get on Ohio Creek?"

"I'm sure you will."

He nodded. "Good." He hated himself for the inability to say what was important. He wanted to reach out to her, but he couldn't. A power much stronger than his heart held him back. Maybe it was better this way—a clean break, a cordial good-bye. It was very modern. Very macho. God, he hated himself for this!

She stood before him tongue-tied, unable to breathe lest she start crying. She was not that sort of woman. She very rarely cried about anything. Why did this man elicit that kind of response from her? Where was her élan, her composure, her cool? Why on earth did she have to act like some tongue-tied schoolgirl who was just suffering from her first adolescent heartbreak! After all, she was a pro at dealing with heartache.

Greg let out a long, ragged breath. "I think I'd better go now, Anne."

"I know," she said.

"I...I don't really know...."

"Good luck with your articles about the mine," she quickly inserted, afraid to let him touch on the sensitive chord that stretched like a too-taut wire between them. "I know they'll be winners."

He paused before answering. "Yeah," he finally said, letting the more emotional moment pass.

"You'll send me a copy of the first article?"

"Sure," he answered.

With a strength that was greater than any she knew she possessed, she stuck out her hand to him. "Well, good-bye, Greg. I wish you the best of everything."

He stared at the outstretched hand and then lifted his eyes to her face, a face held so tight and controlled that the least touch might break it. He wanted to hold her. He wanted to kiss her one more time. But he couldn't do that to her. She was trying so hard to maintain the facade and the control. She was a proud woman and he did not want to be the one to break that spirit in her.

She held out her hand, praying that he wouldn't take it, praying that he would reach for her and make her crumble against him.

She watched with the calmest control as he took her hand and pressed it between his own.

"Good-bye, Anne. I'll keep in touch."

She nodded slowly, afraid to open her mouth to speak, afraid of what she might say in desperation to keep him there one more moment.

He released her hand and bent over for the pack. Slipping one arm through the shoulder harness, he pulled it onto his back and pushed his other arm through the opening. When it was situated properly on his shoulders, he stopped and looked at her for one long, agonizing moment before he turned and started walking down the slope away from the trailer. Away from her.

She watched him go in stoic silence. It was best this way. More practical, more realistic. Their lives were on different planes, going in different directions. They met on a mountainside, they pieced a few moments together between them, and now they would go their own ways. *Yes, Anne. You've always been realistic about life. This is no different.*

She repeated it over and over and almost convinced herself of this while a slim trickle of tears ran down her face. She watched Greg Fisher go until he entered the thick stand of trees and disappeared from her life.

Taking a deep breath to cleanse her lungs and restore her pride, she turned and climbed into the trailer to complete the day's entry in her journal.

Chapter Thirteen

The noise level was at an earsplitting decibel, the laughter moving in waves like rounds of a favorite song, the beer flowing cold and full-bodied and, as Greg would say, Fun spelled with a capital *F*. It was Friday night at the Stable. Directly off campus and with just the right blend of tackiness and chic to hold an appeal for almost everyone, it was Princeton's current "in" place.

There was hardly space to move or breathe in the bar that night, standing room only, the crowd being a mixture of summer school students and those who just seemed to hang around campus on an endless basis.

Greg Fisher was sitting by himself at a booth along the center of the far wall. The noise and gaiety seemed to float around him without touching him. He was staring down at his glass of bourbon—that alone, in a bar whose standard fare was beer, being a telling sign that he was there for the purpose of some serious drinking and was choosing to remain apart from the mad frivolity of the crowd.

He was on his fourth drink in less than an hour, and his mood had sunk lower and lower with each jiggerful. He was dressed like everyone else: gray slacks, Izod shirt, hair short and neatly styled. He fit in as he always had. He was a part of these surroundings and he had accepted that. He had chosen this life fifteen years ago and now he was living with that choice.

Why, then, did he feel so miserably rotten?

His friend, Al Kanook, entered the bar and spotted Greg sitting quietly alone amid the boisterous crowd. Avoiding the busier area around the long bar, he walked over to the booth and sat down. Greg didn't seem to notice that anyone had joined him, so Al sat quietly and studied his friend from across the table.

"So," he said after a couple of minutes, "I understand you didn't find it."

Greg finally looked up and noticed Al sitting there. He reached for a cigarette in his pocket and lit it before answering. "Nope," he said, shaking his head and flipping the match into the ashtray.

Al signaled the waitress for a beer. "Thought for sure you would," he said.

"Yeah, me, too." They were both quiet for a minute while Al paid for his beer and took a drink. Greg downed the rest of his bourbon and ordered another.

"No signs at all of there being a mine up there?"

Greg leaned against the high wooden back of the booth and smoked his cigarette, thinking about a slim fissure in the hard granite, the towering peaks that surrounded a hidden valley, the buildings that had been beaten down by time and winds and reclaimed by the delicate flowers that bloomed in that harsh climate every year. He thought about the graves with their cryptic ideographic markings and the old Chinese man who had raised his pick and sifted through tons of rock for fifty years, knowing with all his heart that untold riches were only the next shovelful away.

On purpose, he excluded any thoughts of Anne in all of the scenes that now drifted before his eyes. He looked back over at Al. "None that I could find," he said and flicked his ashes toward the ashtray.

"You're not going to come through on the Vanguard, are you?"

The waitress set his fifth drink down on the table. Greg saw the worried crease on Al's forehead and took a big drink. "A bet is a bet," he slurred in answer.

Al leaned his elbows on the table. "Come on, Greg, you can't follow through with this. Do you know what will happen to you if anyone finds out? And somewhere down the line, one of those students is bound to let it slip. You know that."

Greg shrugged. "I've never reneged on a bet yet. I don't intend to start now."

Al couldn't hide his frustration. "Think about your career, man! Think about what is important."

Greg chuckled drunkenly at that one. What was important. What a joke! He stubbed out his cigarette and picked up his glass, holding it loosely in his hand. Didn't everyone get it? He, Greg Fisher, Ph.D., didn't have even the faintest idea of what was important anymore.

A couple of girls walked by the booth and he stared at them as they passed. After a minute, one of them came back to his table and stopped. "Hi, Dr. Fisher. Listen, a bunch of us are having a party over at Len Tillman's apartment. You want to come?"

His eyes quickly scanned her face, perfect from the artistry of makeup, and her figure, advertised well in the tight tank top, and he tried not to make comparisons with a strong, slender woman with thick brown hair and brown eyes, with a face free of makeup and artifice, with a perfect body that lay hidden beneath the loose bulk of flannel. He tried not even to think about her, but he was finding that an impossible task. Every moment of the day was filled with comparisons and remembrances, and even massive amounts of alcohol could not make him forget.

"I might stop in for a while," he said to the girl and studied the sway of her hips as she walked back to her table. He chuckled to himself over Al's question and looked over at his friend. "You want to know what's important right now? That little blond coed and her party, that's what."

The creases in Al's forehead deepened. "I heard last night it was a brunette."

"Yeah." Greg's chuckle was without gaiety. "And tomorrow night it just might be a redhead." He stared at his drink in self-disgust, then quickly downed the rest of it and stood up to go. He tried for a smile. "Well," he said to Al. "Looks like it's party time."

IT WAS INDIAN SUMMER, warm and dry and easy, and the late afternoon drifted over and around the two women sitting on the porch drinking lemonade. Anne yawned and stretched in the chaise longue. "Dad doesn't know what he's missing."

Ruth Holdenfield gave a short huff. "That man's memoirs are going to be the death of me yet. Every day it's the same thing. Locks himself in that study to write and rewrite. It must be a twelve-volume set by now. I hate to tell him his life is just not all that interesting." She shook her head in resignation. "But what am I to do?"

Anne laughed lightly and took another sip of her lemonade. "I'd say give up, Mother. You've been working on him all this time and it hasn't made a dent. It doesn't look as if he's going to come out until he's good and ready."

"Well, maybe he'll surprise me like you did. I certainly didn't expect you to leave the mountains in September. And to come here to see us...well, that's almost beyond comprehension!"

"I told you, it started snowing and I just decided I wasn't up to facing that battle yet. Winter is coming early this year. Besides, I was tired. I needed a break."

"I don't doubt it. I can't for the life of me figure how you can stand it up there for so long. Did you do everything you were supposed to do for the study project?"

"Oh, not really," Anne said. "I'll probably have to go back up there when I leave here. There are a couple more areas I need to catalog. I want to describe the migration of the elk as they come down for the winter. And courtship behavior of the sheep should start soon. That's crucial to my study and I don't want to miss it."

"So you won't be here long," her mother said.

"No, not long."

They were silent for several minutes, letting the afternoon settle like a warm sigh around them.

Ruth finally broke the silence. "You want to tell me why you came here, Anne?"

Anne glanced over at her with a startled expression. "What do you mean? I thought you wanted me to come."

"You know I wanted you to. I always want you to. But that hasn't made any big impression on you before."

"Mother!"

"I'm not complaining, dear. I'm just stating the facts. I know you've got your own life and a hundred projects going and it's hard to find the time to get away. I know that and I accept it. But I also can read you like a book. Something is wrong and that's why you're here."

Anne tried to laugh it away. "Everything is fine."

Ruth ignored the denial. "Ever since you came you've been different. Quieter. . .sadder in a way. Even with his head wrapped up in his own life, your father has noticed it. He said as much last night when we were in bed."

Anne stared at her, surprised at her own inability to keep her pain hidden. She thought she had done it very well, but obviously she had not. She closed her eyes and let her head rest against the back of the chaise longue. "I met a man this summer." She shook her head and laughed. "You can't believe this guy, Mother. He is...he is totally the opposite of the type of man I thought I could ever be attracted to."

"Who is he, a forest ranger up there?"

Anne laughed at that one. "Hardly. He's a professor from Princeton."

"Well, what's wrong with that? He sounds perfect for you." Her eyes suddenly narrowed on her daughter. "He isn't married, is he, Anne?"

She shook her head and smiled. "No. He's not the type."

"Then he sounds perfect. Why do you say he's not your type?"

Anne poured another glass of lemonade and took a long sip, thinking about Greg Fisher. "He drinks, he smokes, he gambles away all his money, he dates his students, he thinks women were put on this earth to please him, he—" She chuckled lightly. "He doesn't have a serious bone in his body." She looked up at her mother. "But he made me laugh. He made me feel so different than I had ever felt. And...and I can't get that blasted man out of my mind. I've tried for three months. But damn his hide, I can't stop missing him!"

Ruth studied her daughter closely. "Where is he now?"

Anne shrugged. "Princeton, I suppose. Fall term has started."

"Why don't you go see him?"

Anne looked appalled. "Mother! I am certainly not going to go chasing after some man. We had a summer fling. That's really all it was."

"Is it?"

Anne sighed deeply. "No, not for me, anyway. But it would never work between us. Our work is two thousand miles apart. He teaches on the East Coast, I'm studying here. And once I finish my doctorate, my work will be up in the mountains. There probably aren't too many wildlife ecologists finding work in New Jersey. Besides, he's not the type I could spend my life with."

"He sounds like the type you've been needing all your life, Anne Holdenfield."

Anne looked startled at the didactic tone in her mother's voice.

"Now you listen to me, young lady. You have wasted too many years with men who were about as full of life and color as the concrete floor of this porch. No offense, dear, but that man you were married to was the biggest washout I've ever seen."

"Mother!" she exclaimed, horrified.

"It's true and you know it. Oh, he smiled in public and draped his arm around you and kissed your cheek and put on a great show with you. But he didn't fool me for a minute. The man wouldn't know how to have good sex if his life depended on it."

Anne stared at her mother, unable to believe what she was hearing. But her mother was absolutely correct. "You're right," Anne admitted. "Every man I've ever picked has been a washout."

"For some strange reason you have been under the impression that you have to pick someone exactly like you or the relationship won't work."

Anne laughed. "Are you saying I'm a washout, Mother?"

"No, of course not. I mean you seem to think they have to have this lofty view of the world and be as serious-minded as you all the time. Now you have tried that and you see where it led."

"Yeah, straight to Frank."

"Do you want to know what it takes to keep a relationship or a marriage together?"

"Okay," Anne said with a sigh. "I know you're going to tell me whether I want to know or not."

"It takes fun." She laughed at her daughter's expression. "Yes, dear. Fun. Without that, no couple could stand each other for fifty years...or even five years, for that matter. Look at your father and me. We are nothing alike, and we were nothing alike when we met. But that was the attraction. And it's still the attraction. That man has confounded me and intrigued me and been a challenge to me for forty-five years. That's the only reason I've been able to put up with some of his antics for all these years. He can be a pain in the rear sometimes—like he is right now up there thinking he's Ralph Waldo Emerson. But it's worth it. It's worth the problems, the arguments, the anger, the waiting, because the element of fun has never left us."

"Why didn't you tell me this when I was fifteen?" Anne asked, bewildered by a truth she had never seen.

Ruth Holdenfield smiled. "Because you never would have believed it. You were one of those kids who always had to find her own way with everything. Men were no exception."

"I didn't have any fun with Frank, that's for sure."

"Do you have fun with this professor from Princeton?"

Anne smiled somewhat wickedly. "Do I ever."

"Then do something about it, for heaven's sake."

Anne shook her head. "I don't want to give up my career. I've worked too many years for it."

"Did he ask you to give it up?"

"No."

"Well..."

"I don't know. Maybe it's too late now," Anne thought aloud.

"I would say that's entirely up to you."

She stared out over the lawn, thinking, then turned and smiled at her mother. "Fun, huh?"

Ruth smiled back. "That's right, dear. Fun. With a capital *F*."

"THE VARIOUS TRIBES that developed from these bands took over varying degrees of the southwestern farmers' culture, and also caused the farmers endless trouble." Greg continued to read aloud from his notes. "The Pueblos lived in compact groups in which everyone knew everyone else's business, and each individual was kept exactly in line by the force of unremitting public opinion.... The Navahos wanted no such life. They liked individuality and elbow room, and placed their dwellings accordingly."

Greg stifled a yawn over his own dry recitation, sighed hugely and surveyed the seemingly endless rows of zombies that filled his classroom. Their bodies might be present, but their minds were a thousand light-years away. He noticed one boy doodling on his notebook, so he checked his seating chart for the name.

"Wilson. Philip Wilson."

The kid looked up, startled that he had been picked out of the crowd.

"What was the primary concern of the Navahos?" Greg asked, staring hard at the squirming student.

"Uh...it was...uh...I don't think I read that far."

Greg glared at him for an embarrassing moment, then shifted his attention to a girl on the far side of the room. She was passing a note to the guy behind her. "Allison Bellow."

"Sir?"

"Would you answer the question?"

"What was the question, sir?"

Greg's eyes scanned the room of students who were paying thousands of dollars a year to go to college here but, because they weren't footing the bills, didn't give a damn. He let his hand slap the lectern in front of him. "What is the matter with you people? Where in hell are your minds?"

"I know where mine is," one smart aleck in the back piped up. "But I can't say it in mixed company."

Another got up the courage to speak. "If you'd get off these stale, timeworn lectures, we might wake up."

Greg stared at the kid who had said that. He was slouched in his chair, his hair uncombed, and he was drawing big swirls on the wooden desk with his pen.

"Dr. Fisher," another student ventured. "I sat in on some of your classes last year and they were great.

You had a way of making history come alive. You were always showing ways to live history now and talking about what made certain current events more important historically than others. You really brought it alive. But in this class—''

Greg smirked at the young man and interrupted hotly. ''That's the most ridiculous thing I've ever heard. The whole damn world is falling to pieces around us. Why would any moron want to live that?''

Al Kanook was standing in the doorway of the classroom and he shook his head over what had happened to his friend's attitude. He used to love to sneak into Greg's classes and listen. There was constant electricity about them and a great element of fun. But not now. Not anymore. Now he fully agreed with the students.

''I know what the problem is,'' one kid piped up. ''Ever since Dr. Fisher was passed over for tenure, he's decided he doesn't have to teach anymore.'' A wave of embarrassed laughter rippled through the room following the remark.

Greg slammed his book closed on the lectern. ''All right,'' he growled. ''Since you all seem to be so smart, you can read the next four chapters for Wednesday and be prepared for a test.''

A round of groans and complaints moved across the room as the students closed their notebooks and headed for the door as quickly as they could. Greg's eyes followed them and landed on Al where he was standing just inside the room with his arms folded across his chest. But Greg ignored him and stared down at the book in front of him.

After all the students had gone, Al walked to the front of the room and sat on the edge of a desk while Greg haphazardly crammed his papers into his briefcase.

"Well, well," Al said. "That was very enlightening."

"Shut up."

Al shrugged, knowing that Greg didn't mean anything personal by that. "So," he continued, "how long are you going to keep punishing yourself?"

Greg snapped his briefcase shut. "I'm not punishing myself."

"Really? Sure looks that way when you drink yourself into oblivion every night, smoke at least two packs of cigarettes a day, and spend every last cent you make at the track. And these lectures...how can you do that to yourself? Have you suddenly gone masochistic?"

Greg picked up his briefcase, and the two men left the classroom, walking down the hallway and stairs toward Greg's office. "So what the hell would you do if you lost your chance at tenure?" he snapped.

"Look, I told you what I thought about that. I warned you what could happen if you followed through with the bet. Surely you knew that one of those guys was going to let it slip about how he got into the Vanguard. I told you that."

Al walked along beside him, trying once again to penetrate this new tough veneer his friend was wearing. "But that's not the only reason you're punishing yourself and you know it."

"Oh, do I?" Greg snapped. "How is it that you think you know so much about me anyway?"

"You told me about her."

Greg's head jerked around toward his friend and his eyes held a look of utter surprise.

Al just shrugged. "One night when you were three sheets to the wind," he stated in explanation. "You told me all about Anne Holdenfield."

Greg returned quickly. "So what?"

"So the question is what are you going to do about her?"

"Nothing."

"Why not?"

"Because there is nothing I can do."

Al snorted. "That doesn't sound like the Greg Fisher I know. Hell, I thought the world was yours to own. That's the impression you've always given, you know. The world is one big candy field just waiting for Greg Fisher to gobble it up. What happened to that philosophy?"

"I found out the candy is rotten."

"Doesn't sound to me as if this Anne Holdenfield lady is too rotten. Not from the things you told me anyway."

Greg shifted his briefcase to his other hand. "Look, Al, she's out of my life. Okay? I don't want to talk about her again. Not to you, not to anyone."

Al raised his eyebrows at the snarl in Greg's voice. "Sure, buddy, whatever you say."

They were at his office and Greg was reaching for his key when he saw the piece of paper taped to his door. He reached for it and pulled it down, reading it as he held it in his hands. The writing was small and in a backward slant. "Your velvet cushion was about what I thought it would be—too crowded. If you'd ever care to join me, I'll be back on my pumpkin. Bring one along for yourself."

Greg glanced in the direction they had walked. He turned and looked the other way. His eyes began an almost frantic search of the hallway.

"What is it?" Al asked, reading over Greg's shoulder. "What does that mean?"

Greg's searching gaze stopped on Al's face. "It's her."

"Who?"

"She's been here."

"Who?"

He tore down the hall with Al right behind him, and they dashed down the stairs and to the door of the building. Greg's eyes swept the area around the building, but in the crowd of students he didn't see her. He ran back up the stairs to his office, unlocked the door and hurried to the window, hoping to catch sight of her in that direction.

With his hands against the window frame, he hung his head in frustration.

"Who are you looking for?" Al asked again.

Greg turned around slowly and faced him. "Anne was here. This is from her." He sank to the edge of his desk and stared at the note in his hands.

Al slipped it from Greg's hands and read it again. Then he looked up at Greg and smiled. "So what are you sitting here for, man? For God's sake, get you a pumpkin and go find her."

Chapter Fourteen

The sun was high and bright, but the air was sharp and cold. The aspen had turned to pure gold and the leaves shimmered in the clear morning light. Squirrels busily prepared their nests for winter and chipmunks were engaged in frenzied fall activity. A weasel, completely white now except for a bit of dark down on its back and a black tip on the tail, carried a pika in its mouth. The mountain peaks were dusted with a fine powder of white and streams ran down slow and icy from the higher, ice-covered elevations. The temperature was hovering around the twenty-degree mark, and Greg shivered beneath his heavy down parka.

This time he had rented a car in Gunnison, not wanting to depend on the health situation of Willard Hopkins's family. He rented the car the previous night when he arrived, and left the motel early in the morning. He drove up Ohio Creek Road, following his memory as to the cutoff for Mill Creek Road.

He drove until he could no longer maneuver the car across the ruts and then he parked beside the road. From there, he had started his hike.

But this time he was better prepared. Not only had he provided his own transportation, but he had bought better hiking boots, heavier and more durable clothing, adequate food, fewer packs of cigarettes and only slightly less candy.

He had originally thought that Anne would be back in Boulder by now, but after not finding her and finally reaching her biology department chairman, he had learned that she had come back up to the trailer to finish the year's research. Although the department head had assured Greg that she would be back by November, he wasn't about to wait that long. He was already a fool for waiting as long as he had.

From the moment he left her in June he had known it was a mistake. But what was he to do? He had a job in New Jersey, she had a job here. Their life-styles couldn't be more different or farther apart. And so he had tried to convince himself that theirs had been one of those brief affairs that was definitely worth remembering but not worth pursuing.

How wrong he had been! He had suffered for over three months while he tried to convince himself of that. Nothing had worked. Not drink. Not gambling. Not women. Nothing. He wondered how long he would have gone on had he not received the note from her. Would he, as Al had said, have gone on punishing himself for his own stupidity? Or would he have eventually made some effort to contact her? He really didn't have an answer for that. But he was very grateful that she had at least made the first move.

His life, he realized now, had been one long carnival ride. But he hadn't gone anywhere. He had gone

around and around in circles until all the thrill and
gaiety had wound down and nothing was left but
monotony and endless circling that he couldn't seem
to stop. He wanted the ride to end, but he wasn't sure
how to get off. He had played for the past fifteen
years. He had assumed he would go on playing for the
rest of his life. And, too, he knew that not all of it was
bad. He had had a lot of fun along the way. He had
enjoyed all the parties and the wagers and the dares—
that much would probably never change. But he was
tired of having nothing else.

Anne Holdenfield was the first person who had
ever shown him that there could be something else for
him. She was a challenge that had been lacking in his
life. She was a dare that offered a much more sub-
stantial reward at the end. She had a dedication that
he admired, a strength that he found comforting
without feeling threatened, a femininity that had
haunted and enticed him for the past three months,
driving him almost to the brink of distraction at times.
She offered a balance that had been missing in his life.
She gave stability where he was weak, soft yielding
where he was strong and a stubborn streak that he
would never tire of chipping away at.

The big question was how was she going to feel
about all of this. She had left him a note, true. But she
had not stayed around to pursue it very far. That was
what he had to find out. That was what he had to work
on. And as she surely knew by now, he was a persist-
ent nuisance when it came to getting what he wanted.
Yes, Anne Holdenfield had better watch out, because Greg Fisher was on his way. And he hadn't

come up here on this little hike for the fun of it, either. Mountain climbing was never going to be a sport for him. It would probably always remain pure torture.

As he hiked he recognized the landmarks he had passed on his trip in June. But nature had a way of changing the panorama so that, at every turn, he saw something new. He saw snow where three months ago wild hyacinth and coralroot had grown, bare white trunks of aspen trees where quaking green leaves had been. There were places where porcupines had been stripping the bark from the lower branches of limber pine, where red squirrels had assembled middens for the long winter ahead. Blue jays still chattered in the trees above, but there was more of a method to their madness now, as if they, too, were signaling the approach of hard times.

He stopped for lunch by a creek and refilled his canteen. The motel had once again packed a nice picnic of roast beef sandwiches, carrot sticks, a plum and a large Hershey's bar. He ate it all and drank lots of the cool, clear water from the icy creek.

It was shortly after noon when he made it to the trailer, and he could tell immediately that she wasn't there. No fire was lit, and the place had a closed-up look about it. He knocked, knowing it was a waste of time, but he did it anyway. When she didn't answer, he tried to hide his disappointment as he looked around her small camp. A pair of jeans hung on the line she had strung between the trees. He dropped his pack to the ground, then walked over and touched the jeans, as if by doing so he would be touching her. They were dry but cold, and he took them down and folded them up, laying them on the table by her Coleman stove and coffeepot.

There were only cold dregs in the pot, so he carried it to the stream and washed it out, replacing it with fresh water and the small packet of fresh coffee grounds he had brought with him. He turned on the stove and heated the coffee, then pulled a cup from his pack to pour in the hot liquid. He sat down on a boulder, the one on which he had sat that first day when she was pointing a rifle at him, and slowly sipped the coffee, letting the steaming liquid warm his body for the first time all day.

He knew there was nothing to do but wait until Anne came back. She was probably out chasing after her sheep again. He smiled at the image of her creeping across the rocky ledges, scanning with her scope every high grassy bench where the sheep might be grazing. He thought of Solomon and Sheba for the first time since the summer and he wondered what had happened to them. He would have to remember to ask her if she had seen them again.

He wanted to ask her so many things, he didn't even know where to begin. How did you go about telling a woman like Anne you love her, that you can't live without her, that if you don't make love to her again you are going to go stark raving mad? He had never felt that way about any woman, much less felt the need to inform her about it. But somehow that was exactly what he had to do.

He finished his coffee and picked up his pack, carrying it some fifty feet away to the spot where he had camped before. He loosened his tent from the frame and started the laborious task of figuring out how to set the darn thing up. He didn't know how long Anne would be gone. She could be out just for the day or she could be camping out. He would wait; however long it took, he would wait.

THE HERD WAS PLACID for now, feeding on all the herbs and grasses they could get before the winter snows covered the ground. Anne sat on a rimrock overlooking the valley below. Her movie camera was on her shoulder and she had already gotten several feet of their quiet behavior. There wasn't much vegetation here, and this was a broad, open area with branches, ridgetops and saddles, and she had to stay down low against the rocks so as not to be seen. Two ewes and a lamb climbed the rocky cliff and stopped in the saddle where she was sitting. They saw her instantly, spooked and then tore down the mountainside with the rest of the herd following close behind.

With a sigh, she packed up her binoculars and camera equipment and started the long, arduous hike back to her trailer. It had snowed several times already that month, and the ground was dotted with patches of white that would not melt until spring. She crossed two sets of tracks, indicating that a coyote had stalked a ptarmigan, but the bird had lost the hunt just as it reached its snow roost. Bear tracks, too, were more noticeable now in the soft mounds of snow, as were the tracks of deer and elk. And only that morning she had seen two bull elk coming out of the trees near Willow Lake.

She lifted her pack higher onto her shoulder and breathed in the fresh cold air as she hiked. She would soon be leaving for the winter and she had mixed feelings about it. She would miss the peace and solitude, miss the quiet dignity and majesty of the animals, the freshness of the air, the ever-changing colors of the landscape. At the same time she needed a change of pace. Too many memories that were best forgotten lay here in these mountains. By next summer she would be over him completely...or so she kept telling herself. She would be able to come back to her work, fresh and whole once again. A new year, a new season of wildlife, a new beginning. She would concentrate on her thesis this winter and, she hoped, would not have enough time to think about Greg Fisher.

Even now, when she thought about what she had done after leaving her parents' house, she was flushed with embarrassment. Leaving that note for him was foolish. He would think she was some sort of crazy schoolgirl who had a hopeless crush on him. He and his friends would no doubt have a good laugh over it. And yet at the time it had seemed the right thing to do. She had to make an effort. That way she could not blame herself for letting the relationship slide away. It would be all him. He would be responsible for her pain. She would be free to hate him and then get over him. So despite her embarrassment over the note, her conscience was at least at ease now.

While she was hiking, she had been thinking about her thesis, about the next few sections she would have

to write when she got back to Boulder, about the
questions she needed to ask her professor.

She had so many things on her mind that she was
halfway through the clearing before she noticed the
tent. She stopped and frowned, as if a mirage had
suddenly sprung up from the meadow floor. She
blinked several times, but the image remained. The
tent was blue. It was sitting crooked. It was his.

Her heart began a wild staccato beat as she stood
knee deep in sedge and wild rye. A few lingering
flowers had braved autumn, clinging tenaciously to
their last few days of color. She tried to tell herself to
be calm, not to presume too much, but the words did
not stick for long. Her heart continued to pound, her
pulse raced and her body reacted curiously by rapidly heating up only to be covered by goose bumps.

She forced her feet to move and she slowly made her
way across the clearing, drawing nearer to the spot
where he had made camp. She carefully removed her
pack and set it on the ground.

He was coming out of the woods with a pan of
water from the creek when he saw her. She was
standing ten feet from the tent, staring at the campsite he had worked so hard all morning to set up. Her
head lifted and she saw him. Neither moved for a few
seconds as they drank in the sight of each other from
a distance.

There was caution in her stance, a caution that de-
nied all the wild longings that raced through her body
at the mere sight of him, standing there with the sun
on his hair, the sky in his eyes and a smile that ignited
a spark of fire deep within her.

He shifted the pan of water to his other hand and moved toward her. She was even more beautiful than he had remembered. Like fall, her colors had changed with the evolving season. Her eyes appeared browner, her hair shinier, with highlights of red that he had never noticed before. She wore a down vest over a plaid blouse, and her jeans hugged her curves in such a way that he thought he might explode with the need he had for her right then.

He set the pot of water down on the ground by the fire and stepped up to her. She was watching him in silence, a stunned look on her face, as if she truly had believed she would never see him again, as if he had died and now suddenly returned to life.

Unable to stand it any longer, he reached for her, and she fell into the waiting warmth of his arms. No words passed between them. No words were needed. His mouth, warm and open over hers, and his hands roaming hard and possessively under her down vest, said it all. He pulled her tight against him and she could feel how badly he wanted her. She pressed against him, loving the feel of his body as she moved her hands over his back and hips.

His mouth moved to her neck and her head fell back against the cup of his hand. She tried to catch her breath, but the thin air mixed with her burning desire would not let her. "Why...why are you here?" she asked, gasping, weak from the touch of his fingers moving like flames of fire between them, covering her breasts, her neck, between her thighs.

"Because I can't stay away," he told her, yanking her down vest off her shoulders and throwing it to the ground. His fingers were frantic against the buttons of her shirt, and he ended up ripping two of them off as he quickly removed her shirt.

"Greg..."

"No, not now," he commanded harshly, pulling her hips up against his thighs. He held her that way for a long moment, very still, without speaking. Then, loosening his hold for only a moment, he flipped back the flap on the tent and pulled her inside and lowered her to the waiting bedroll.

Following her down to the sleeping bag, he propped himself up on his elbow beside her and gazed down at her, his breath ragged and quick inside the warm tent. His hand reached out slowly to touch her breasts, almost tentatively this time, as if he could not believe she was actually there with him, lying beside him, waiting for his possession.

She stared back at him, her breath suspended in the drama of waiting for his touch, waiting for her body to be captured up in his talons.

His head dropped down to her stomach, his mouth and tongue gliding along the line at the top of her jeans. His hand moved between her thighs, his fingers probing against the unyielding material.

And then suddenly all patience was gone from them both. Her hand reached for his and guided it to the snap at her waist and he tore the jeans open, pulling them roughly over her hips. She sat up with him and removed her underwear while he unbuttoned his shirt. She helped him pull it off, running her hands across the hard flesh of his chest, wanting to feel the warmth of it against her own.

He removed the rest of his clothes in a matter of seconds and, with his hands on her shoulders, pressed her back against the down bedding beneath them, followed the pull of her hands against the back of his neck and covered her body with his own.

A pine grosbeak finch, perched on a log outside the tent, fluttered and trilled to the glory of the magnificent fall afternoon, while inside the tent Greg and Anne gloried in the magnificence of each other's arms.

Later, curved against each other beneath the cover for warmth, Anne ran her fingers lightly along his chest. "Am I dreaming this?" she asked. "If I am, please don't wake me."

He kissed the damp hair at her temple, swallowed the lump of emotion that filled his chest to overflowing. "The note, Anne.... Why didn't you stay and wait for me? Why the note and not you?"

She closed her eyes as caution began once more to wind its tight band around her heart. "I was afraid, Greg."

He tilted his head so that he could see her face. "Of what? Me?"

She kept her eyes on his chest. "Of me. Of...of the way I feel."

"How do you feel?" he asked earnestly.

"I think you know."

"Could you say it? Please." There was a brief span of silence. "It would mean a lot to me."

She finally looked up, wariness clouding the autumn lights in her eyes. She swallowed hard. "I love you, Greg." It was uttered reluctantly, hesitantly, through tight lips. But it was uttered.

He pulled her close and held her within the large circle of his arms. "I love you, too, Anne. I haven't been able to get you off my mind for a minute. And believe me, I've tried." He pulled back and looked down into her face once more. "I've tried everything...with everyone."

She knew what he was telling her. He was telling her that he had tried to use others to forget her. At the thought of him with other women a sharp pain stabbed through her. But then, if she had had the opportunity, wouldn't she have done the same? Wouldn't she have done anything to erase him from her mind? After all, she had used sex with him as a tool to loosen his hold over her. That plan had failed, but she might have tried it again.

"Why are we doing this to ourselves?" she moaned, sitting up in the sleeping bag and reaching for her underwear and jeans. "Why are we prolonging this agony?" She looked back down at him. "There is no way for this to work, Greg. You know it and I know it, so who are we trying to fool?"

He reached over and rested his hand on her waist. "All I know, Anne, is that I can't stay away from you. I can't do it."

She hung her head and expelled a tired, uneven breath, then pulled her legs free of the cover and dressed. She crawled out of the tent and found her shirt, slipping it on and fastening what few buttons were left.

Greg came out of the tent, fastening his jeans and holding his shirt in his hand. "Why are you fighting this?" he asked. "You're the one who came to Princeton and left the note. You're just as miserable as I am, so why are you fighting it?"

"Because it can't work."

"Why can't it?"

She tilted her head back and closed her eyes. Facing him once again, she answered. "I came to Princeton to see if I could live there. I can't."

"You didn't even give it a chance."

"I don't want to give it a chance, Greg. This is where I want to be. This is where my work is. I can't change that. I don't want to change it." She studied the sullen expression on his face. "I could say the same thing to you, you know. I could ask you why you don't give up your teaching career in the East and move out here and live up in the mountains with me in the summer."

He regarded her for a moment, then let out a short, cynical breath. "I couldn't do that. I...it's...this isn't me."

"I know you couldn't, Greg," she said in all sincerity. "This isn't you any more than New Jersey is me. You have a wonderful career. I don't want to mess that up for you."

"Not so wonderful." It came out as a grumble.

"Greg, to receive tenure at Princeton is a great position to be in."

"I was passed over."

"Your career is set and—What did you say?"

"I said I was passed over."

She was very still as she watched him slip on his shirt and button it. "What do you mean? I thought it was a sure thing. I thought the discovery of the mine and the articles would cinch it."

He walked over to the fire pit and struck a match to light the tinder flakes he had placed under the logs earlier. "There were no articles. There was no discovery."

She followed him and sat down on a log across from him, her puzzled eyes never leaving his face. "I don't understand."

Sitting down, he rested his elbows on the tops of his thighs and stared at the stick he was now beating against a rock. "I couldn't do it, Anne. I couldn't do it to that old man up there."

"Lin Chung?"

He nodded. "That place is his whole life. To take that away from him would be like...like murder almost." He looked over at her. "I couldn't have lived with myself if I had done it. Someday maybe, when he's gone...if no one else has discovered it yet, I'll go back up there. And then maybe I'll write about it. I don't know."

Anne blinked back the tears that began to well up in her eyes and throat, then swallowed. "And the bet?"

He shrugged. "I lost it."

"But what about your debts?"

"I'll just have to pay them off the way everybody else pays off bad debts: slowly and painfully."

"When did you decide that you couldn't reveal the secret of the mine?"

He was silent for a brief moment. "That day we talked to Lin Chung."

"When you told me to wait and you walked back over to him," she said, almost in a daze, remembering that she had felt so left out, so rejected. "Did you tell him then that you weren't going to say anything about it?"

"Yes."

They were both silent for a few minutes while the fire took hold and crackled hot against the early evening chill.

Anne looked up, startled as a thought struck her. "The Vanguard! The bet you made with the students...did you have to...you didn't go through with it, did you?" The look on his face was all the answer she needed. "Oh, Greg!"

The stick snapped as it hit the rock. He laughed, but the sound was harsh and grating. "I've been in a self-destruct mode for so long. I suppose this was just the final blow."

"Couldn't you just have refused to—" She saw the look on his face. "No, I guess you couldn't."

"When you gamble, you take the losses with the wins."

"Did your tenure committee find out? Is that why you were passed over?"

He pressed his lips together and nodded. "I'd say my career at Princeton is going to be a short-lived one."

"Have you thought of applying to another college...one out here maybe?" She held her breath as she watched him sitting so still, staring at the fire.

He finally looked up. "Like the University of Colorado?"

She nodded, afraid to breathe.

"That might take time," he said, clearly understanding her meaning. If he were here, they would at least be closer. "It won't solve everything, you know."

"Yes, I know."

"I still have to finish out this year at Princeton."

"I know," she said again, not wanting to hope for too much.

"I might not be accepted at Boulder."

"Maybe not."

"I might end up in Timbuktu."

"You might."

The afternoon waned around them, golden glow faded to rose and purple. The air grew cooler, the breeze stilled, and the songs of the birds diminished with the fading light.

Greg glanced up sharply, his eyes suddenly bright with a newfound optimism. "I've got a great idea, Anne. Let's get married."

She stared back at him, her expression incredulous. "What?"

"Let's get married."

"Married? How could we. . .that would never work."

He moved over to the log beside her and took her hands, his eyes positively glittering with this new brilliant notion of his. "It would work, Anne. Think about it. People have long-distance relationships all the time. We could fly back and forth to see each other.''

"Every night?" she asked with a laugh.

He laughed with her. "I guess with us that would be the temptation, wouldn't it?"

She turned her face away from him, all humor gone for the moment. "I couldn't share you, Greg."

He sat very still.

"I couldn't bear the thought of you being with other women."

"I don't want to be with anyone else, Anne. I...can't...be with..." He let out a slow, labored breath. "Those other women I was with. . ." He cleared his throat a couple of times. "This is really difficult for me to say, but I, uh, couldn't do...I wasn't able to...I was...Damn, I can't say the word!"

"Impotent?"

"Shhh!" he whispered. "Not so loud."

She stared at the frown on his face, aware of the utter bewilderment that he, a man who had been a sexual aggressor all his life, must be feeling. She smiled and threw her arms around his shoulders. "You didn't do anything with those other women?"

She felt him shake his head within the circle of her arms. He pulled back and finally looked her in the eyes. "I couldn't, Anne. I kept seeing you and wanting to be with you. No one else came close."

She hugged him tightly again and planted kisses all over his face and neck. "This is crazy, Fisher. You know that, don't you? I must be crazy to even consider it."

"Then you'll marry me?" he asked.

"Oh, I don't know...."

"Please. I love you, Anne."

"It might not work."

"It will. I promise you. Besides, we're both miserable apart now. We might as well at least be married and be miserable apart."

She made a face. "That doesn't make a whole hell of a lot of sense, you know."

"Nothing does, Anne. The fact that we met doesn't make sense. The fact that we can't be together doesn't make sense. The only thing that makes any sense at all is that we love each other."

She rested the top of her head against his chest and shook her head. "I have definitely lost my mind."

"I can take that as yes, then?"

She looked up at him. "Yes. Yes, you crazy, lovable nut. Yes, yes, yes!"

Greg stood up and picked her up in his arms and swung her around and around as he held her. "It's going to be great, Anne," he said when he brought her back to the ground. "I promise you that we'll have the best marriage anyone ever had."

Practical to the very end, Anne placed her hands on his jaw, her expression steady with a caution she could not cast to the wind quite so easily. "I spend my summers up here, Greg. I don't want to give that up."

"I know that. I don't expect you to."

"And once I start working for the Forest Service, I might be up here a lot in the winter, too."

"We'll send love notes via snow geese. We'll send smoke signals. We'll work it out, Anne. And I'm not saying that I'll never come back up to these mountains, either." He looked around at the darkening evening. "This place has kind of grown on me—sort of."

She laughed. "You may just become a mountain man yet."

"Don't hold your breath."

"I won't." She suddenly grew serious again. "I need space, Greg. I need a lot of it in my life. I'm used to living alone, doing things my way."

"Would you stop worrying so much. Listen, Anne, I know you need space. So do I. But from the sound of this arrangement, it looks like we'll be living alone a good deal of the time."

She sighed deeply. "Are we crazy or what, Greg Fisher?"

He looped his arms around her waist. "Crazy in love with each other."

"I do love you, you know. I've never felt about anyone the way I feel about you."

He puffed out his chest. "Well, I'm that kind of guy."

"Oh, please," she said with a groan, pushing away from him and standing up. "What have I gotten myself into?" *A lifetime of fun, Anne, that's what,* she said to herself. *The challenge will never end.*

She glanced toward a rock at the edge of the fire, then at Greg, then back at the rock. "Is that my coffeepot?"

"Yes."

She raised her eyebrows. "You certainly made yourself at home, didn't you? I don't suppose I could trouble you for a cup, could I?"

"Certainly, my dear." He stood up and reached for a cup, filling it with coffee. "It's warm."

"Are you hungry? Oh, dumb question, Anne. Of course he's hungry. Jack Bennett gave me some venison. Want to try a stew?"

"Sounds great. I'll take anything but one of these packets of freeze-dried soy things." He reached for her hand. "But first there's something I want to do before it gets too dark."

"What?" He dragged her behind him. "Where are we going?"

He led her through the trees and toward the creek. "I know the perfect spot. I found it when I was gathering firewood earlier."

"Found what? Perfect spot for what? Where are you taking me?"

He helped her across the creek by stepping on partially submerged boulders, then led her up over a small rocky hill and up farther to a grassy knoll that overlooked a small valley below. It was rapidly growing darker, so he forced her to walk faster. "Hurry, before the light is gone."

"I'm hurrying, I'm hurrying."

They finally reached a plateau covered in soft grasses and overlooking a meadow far below. A creek meandered through it and, in the soft light of the late afternoon, it washed over the rocks like molten silver.

"What do you think?"

She looked up at him. "I think it's beautiful but...why are we here?"

"We're going to get married."

"Here?"

"Yes."

"Now?"

"Yes." He noticed her stern expression. "Now don't go all proper on me, Anne. I'll fly out from New Jersey when you come down from the mountain and we'll make it legal. But for now, I want to do this. I don't want to wait another month."

She reached up and touched his jaw, smiling. "You are really a wonderful man, did you know that? I think this is a great idea."

"Good." He faced her, took her hands and started to speak, but he stopped suddenly and frowned. "Do you know what we're supposed to say? How do these things go?"

She laughed and lifted his hands to her mouth, kissing the backs of each one. "I say, Greg Fisher do you take me to be your lawful wedded wife, to have and to hold from this day forward, for better or for worse, in sickness and in health, till death do us part?"

He smiled down into the brown glow of her eyes. "I do."

"Good. Now you say it to me."

"Okay. Ah…Anne Holdenfield, do you take me to be your…ah…"

"Lawful wedded husband."

"Lawful wedded husband," he repeated. "To have and to hold forever…is that right?"

"Close enough," she said, a smile stretched across her face.

"In sickness and in health, for better or worse, till death do us part?"

Her brown eyes washed across his face and centered on his blue ones. "Oh, yes, I do."

Greg let go of her hands and pulled her to him, his mouth brushing across the soft line of her forehead. "Then I pronounce us man and wife," he whispered lovingly.

She pressed her lips against his neck, drowning in the warmth of his arms. "You may kiss the bride," she told him, and her breath was stolen from her lungs as he did just that, lifting her in his arms and lowering her to the grassy knoll of dense reddish gold foxtail barley.

And in the valley far, far below them, hidden beneath an overlying rim of rock, Solomon approached a cautious Sheba, touched her gently on her hind leg with his front hoof. She skittishly jumped aside, ran a few yards and then stopped, waiting for him to approach again.

For this was October, and the mating season had begun.

Epilogue

Anne stuck out her hand and took the stick Greg held out to her. "What is this, Fisher?"

"A sparkler."

"What for?"

"It's Fourth of July. Down on the flat, we're all celebrating with firecrackers and chicken and watermelon and all that stuff. You remember. . .Independence Day? United States of America?"

She laughed. "I remember, I remember. Here let me help you take your pack off. Good grief, what do you have in here that's so heavy, a case of Milky Ways?"

"Nah, Snickers. I'm sick of Milky Ways. Ever since I've been trying to stop smoking, all I do is eat." He removed his pack and leaned it against the log cabin. "So this is where they've stashed you, huh?"

"Yep. It's an old miner's cabin. What do you think?"

He leaned a hand against the cabin and stared down
at his wife, studying her every feature. "I think it's
kind of rustic for someone in your condition."

She reached up and kissed him. "I'm fine, really I
am. Don't be such a worrywart."

"I can't help but worry."

"Look, Greg, think of all those Indian squaws who
used to roam all over these mountains pregnant. They
managed fine."

"But they weren't my wife." He reached out and
touched her hair. "God, I've missed you!"

She wrapped her arms around his waist and held
him tight. "And I've missed you more than you can
imagine. It's been such a long month." Still holding
on to him, she looked up. "Did you get settled in your
new office?"

"Yeah. It's bigger than the one I had at Princeton.
I've got a window that looks out over the Wasatch
Range. It's really beautiful."

"University of Utah," she mused softly. "Well, it's
not Colorado, but it's at least closer than New
Jersey."

"It's going to be a great position. I think I'm going
to like it."

Her grin turned positively mischievous as she
peered up at him.

He narrowed his eyes on her. "What are you grinning about? What have you got up your sleeve?"

"Oh, nothing much," she said, drawing out the
suspense for as long as she could. "It's just that I've

been talking to the Fish and Game director in Utah and they're wanting to implement a special study on the bighorn up in the high Uintas and they...well, they asked me to head it up."

Greg's mouth fell open as he stared down at her. "Are you kidding me? You're serious!"

She nodded happily.

"Anne, that's great!" He picked her up and swung her around.

"Put me down before I have the baby in midair."

He set her down gently. "That's wonderful, Anne. We'll be together finally. In the same state. I can't believe it. Listen, I found this great old house near campus. You're going to love it. I just know it."

"Are you going to be able to stand being around me that much?"

"I'm tough," he said. "I think I can endure it."

"Oh, and guess what?" she cried excitedly. "I forgot to tell you. Remember the lamb that Sheba had in March?"

"Yes. Did it make it?"

"Yes. I saw it for the first time the other day. He's already becoming a regular member of the herd. And he chases all the ewes around, too nibbling on their flanks or kicking at their hind legs."

"Sounds like he's a chip off the old block."

"Speaking of chips off the old block, we never decided what we're going to name this one."

He smiled slowly and ran his hand down the side of her hair and onto her shoulder. "Well, maybe we'd better go inside now and work on that." His voice was low and warm as he drew her close. "I hope to hell you have a bed in there."

Her hands rested on his chest and she slowly unfastened the top button of his shirt. "I thought you wanted to work on a name for the baby."

"Oh, I do," he whispered, scooping her up in his arms and carrying her toward the door while his eyes traveled hungrily over her body. "But first things first," he said, kicking open the door. "I made a bet with myself to see how long I could be with you without making love to you."

She laughed and smiled up at him. "And?"

He slammed the door shut behind them and followed her down onto the soft four-poster, his voice a low, husky growl. "I just lost the bet."

She fought for a bold future until she could no longer ignore the...

ECHO OF THUNDER

MAURA SEGER

Author of **Eye of the Storm**

ECHO OF THUNDER is the love story of James Callahan and Alexis Brockton, who forge a union that must withstand the pressures of their own desires and the challenge of building a new television empire.

Author Maura Seger's writing has been described by *Romantic Times* as having a "superb blend of historical perspective, exciting romance and a deep and abiding passion for the human soul."

The final book in the trilogy by

MAURA SEGER

EDGE OF DAWN

The story of the Callahans and Garganos concludes as Matthew and Tessa must stand together against the forces that threaten to destroy everything their families have built.

From the unrest and upheaval of the sixties and seventies to the present, *Edge of Dawn* explores a generation's coming of age through the eyes of a man and a woman determined to love no matter what the cost.

COMING IN FEBRUARY 1986

EDG-H-1

You're invited to accept 4 books and a surprise gift **Free!**

Acceptance Card

Mail to: Harlequin Reader Service®

In the U.S.
2504 West Southern Ave.
Tempe, AZ 85282

In Canada
P.O. Box 2800, Postal Station A
5170 Yonge Street
Willowdale, Ontario M2N 6J3

YES! Please send me 4 free Harlequin American Romance® novels and my free surprise gift. Then send me 4 brand new novels as they come off the presses. Bill me at the low price of $2.25 each —an 11% saving off the retail price. There are no shipping, handling or other hidden costs. There is no minimum number of books I must purchase. I can always return a shipment and cancel at any time. Even if I never buy another book from Harlequin, the 4 free novels and the surprise gift are mine to keep forever.

154 BPA-BPGE

Name	(PLEASE PRINT)	

Address		Apt. No.

City	State/Prov.	Zip/Postal Code

This offer is limited to one order per household and not valid to present subscribers. Price is subject to change.
ACAR-SUB-1

Readers rave about Harlequin American Romance!

"...the best series of modern romances
I have read...great, exciting, stupendous,
wonderful."
— S.E.,* Coweta, Oklahoma

"...they are absolutely fantastic...going to be
a smash hit and hard to keep on the
bookshelves."
— P.D., Easton, Pennsylvania

"The American line is great. I've enjoyed
every one I've read so far."
— W.M.K., Lansing, Illinois

"...the best stories I have read in a long
time."
— R.H., Northport, New York

*Names available on request.

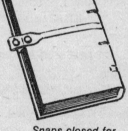